MEASURE, MEASURE!

A Bangzi Opera adapted from
William Shakespeare's
Measure for Measure

by
Ching-Hsi Perng and Fang Chen
English Translation by Ching-Hsi Perng

STUDENT BOOK CO., LTD.

MEASURE, MEASURE!
A Bangzi Opera adapted from
William Shakespeare's *Measure for Measure*
by Ching-Hsi Perng and Fang Chen
English Translation by Ching-Hsi Perng

Copyright©**Student Book Co., Ltd.** 2012
All rights reserved.
No.11, Lane 75, Sec. 1, He-Ping E. Rd., Taipei, Taiwan
http://www.studentbook.com.tw
email: student.book@msa.hinet.net

ISBN 978-957-15-1564-9

Translator's Note:

Once again, with great pleasure and most sincere gratitude
I record here my indebtedness to a long-time friend
and Shakespearean scholar,
Professor Tom Sellari, of National Chengchi University, Taipei,
Taiwan, who went over an earlier version
of the English translation
with loving care and critical acumen,
and offered a wealth of useful suggestions for improvement,
most of which have been incorporated here.
Any infelicities that remain are of course
solely my responsibility.

Measure, Measure! was premiered on 8 June 2012 at National Theatre, Taipei, Taiwan. It was produced by Taiwan Bangzi Company in association with Voices of Spring Symphony Orchestra.

Director	*Po-Shen LU*
Associate Director	*Ching-Chun YIN*
Conductor	*Yung-Ching CHEN*
Composer	*Yuqing GENG*
Arrangement	*Hongquan LI*
Costume Design	*Yu-Sheng LI*
Stage Design	*Ron CHANG*
Light Design	*JACK*
The Prince / Priest Wen	*Hai-Ling WANG*
Murong Qing	*Yang-Ling HSIAO*
An Qilo	*Chian-Hua LIU*
Quan Shike	*Hai-Shan CHU*
Lord Dian	*Ching-Chun YIN*
Fu Qiaoyin	*Wen-Chi HSIEH*
Murong Bai	*Yi-Sheng CHANG*
Master Qiu	*Yung-Wei LIN*
Lu Qiu	*Hsiao-Wei CHENG*
Madam	*Yang-Chen HSIAO*

Xiang Yu	*Chang-Min HU*
Ho Baosheng	*Yuan-Ching YANG*
Prostitutes	*Jui-Yun FU*
	Yang-Lang CHANG
	Yi-Ting SUN
	Mei-Ling CHEN
Whoremasters	*Yang-Chuan CHANG*
	Yuan-Mao LIN
	Yuan-Chin YANG

List of Characters

THE PRINCE	The Prince of Nanping
MURONG QING	Elder sister of MURONG BAI, a novice of Daoism
AN QILO	Lord Protector of Nanping during the Prince's absence
QUAN SHIKE	Prime minister of Nanping
LORD DIAN	Minister of Justice, also in charge of prison affairs
FU QIAOYIN	Younger sister of General Fu and formerly betrothed to AN QILO
MURONG BAI	From a literary family whose fortune has fallen
MASTER QIU	Head priest of Chongxu Daoist Temple
PRIEST WEN	A wandering Daoist monk (disguised by the Prince of Nanping)
LU QIU	A dandy
MADAM	Owner of House of Pleasant Spring, a house of prostitution
XIANG YU	A pimp and bartender
HE BAOSHENG	A headsman

Some prostitutes

Some Whoremasters

Some civilians

Some attendants

Some officers

List of Scenes

Prologue

Location: A thoroughfare in Nanping

(*A crowd gesticulates while watching the newly posted notice on the bulletin board.*)

[Chorus, *offstage*]:

In secrecy the Prince has left the capital.

His sub, the Lord Protector, a strict legalist,

Will prosecute the law without remorse.

A sudden, fright'ning change!—Is this for real?

A sudden, fright'ning change!—Is this for real?

Scene 1: Breaking the Law

(immediately following the Prologue)

LU QIU: My! All the brothels in town will be torn down, not a brick
remaining!

WHOREMASTER 1: Hey, look what it says here: even the policy
of "One beauty per building" has been revoked. . . .

WHOREMASTER 2: Isn't this too severe? Tell me, is it for real this
time?

WHOREMASTER 1: Who knows! Has His Majesty seen this notice?

LU QIU: Of course not! He is abroad on a secret diplomatic
mission—

CROWD: What secret? What diplomacy?

WHOREMASTER 1: How do *you* know?

LU QIU: Humph! What is there that I, Lu Qiu, don't know? His
Majesty is as busy as a bee at this moment. He is banding
with the princes of East Hua and West Qi in a negotiation
with the King of North Tang. Unless a deal is struck, they
will soon attack North Tang.

MADAM: Ay! Thus, what with the war, the plague, and the tearing down of houses, my business is done for.

PROSTITUTE 1: You said it. The rich Master Guo has not been seen for half a month, and Master Cai is nowhere to be found. . . . They used to come every day!

PROSTITUTE 2: And now, even Pockmark Wang finds it profitless to hawk Viagra here.

MADAM: Why, here's a change indeed! What shall become of me?

LU QIU: Come! Fear not! You can simply change the name "House of Pleasant Spring" and carry on the old business. Change it, say, to "Mansion of Rejuvenation"—same old stuff with a different label!

(*Enter* XIANG YU, *the pimp, running.*)

XIANG YU: Madam! (*breathless*) Yonder, yonder (*points to the stage entrance*) is a man arrested!. . .

MADAM: Calm down! Who is it?

XIANG YU: It's Young Master Murong!

CROWD: (*surprised, all at the same time*) What? Young Master Murong?

MADAM: He's worth five thousand of you all! (*to* XIANG YU) Are you sure?

XIANG YU: Of course! I was plying my wares on Outer Street by the gate when I saw with my own eyes Lord Dian order him arrested. What's more, I heard that his head is to be chopped off within three days!

CROWD: (*frightened, all at the same time*) What? His head to be chopped off?

LU QIU: No wonder then.—He promised to meet me two hours since, and he was ever precise in promise-keeping.

MADAM: (*to* XIANG YU) What has he done?

XIANG YU: A woman.

LU QIU: What was his offense?

XIANG YU: He shouldn't have groped for trout in a private stream. The girl is . . . (*He mimes a big belly.*)

LU QIU: Pregnant, eh? Even such fooling doesn't deserve decapitation, does it?

CROWD: (*nodding agreement*) No, of course not!

MADAM: Right! What does that matter? When my girls here get pregnant by accident, I send the kids to our affiliated nursery—a fringe benefit of our enterprise . . .

(*Noise from the entrance door; everyone turns to look.*)

XIANG YU: Hey, look! Isn't that Master Murong?

(*Enter* LORD DIAN, *the Minister of Justice, with two* OFFICERS *leading* MURONG BAI.)

MURONG BAI: Your Honor, why this fuss—showing me thus in a cangue to the world? Just take me to the prison.

LORD DIAN: Master Murong, I do it not out of malice, but by special order of the Lord Protector.

MURONG BAI: Well, one who wields power is like a demigod. At his mercy is the life of the offender. On whom it will, it will. However he judges, he is always right. Alas!

LU QIU: (*rushes up, bowing incessantly to* LORD DIAN) My lord, please allow me to say a few words to him.

(LORD DIAN *gestures permission and steps back.*)

LU QIU: (*to* MURONG BAI) How now, my dear friend? How come you've fallen into this disgrace?

MURONG BAI: Ah, from too much liberty, Brother Lu. A bit of carelessness results in offense. Like rats that devour poison and then die, in pursuit of pleasure we forget restraint.

LU QIU: (*aside*) Ha! How wisely he speaks even under arrest . . . bookish fool! (*to* MURONG BAI) What exactly is your offense?

MURONG BAI: Ah, Brother Lu—as you know, my cousin and I were prenatally betrothed to each other, but for lack of money we have delayed the marriage. Who'd have known that a moment's trick would lead to pregnancy . . . .?

LU QIU: Well, get married then, thus cementing an old tie. It's no big deal.

MURONG BAI: That was my plan. But before I could offer the
bridegroom's gifts, this Lord Protector promulgated these
severe laws and I stand charged with lechery.

LU QIU: A new official has to make his mark, eh?

MURONG BAI: You said it. The Lord Protector—

(*sings*)

> **New in office and in brand-new robe,**
>
> **He rules with unrelenting tyranny.**
>
> **How effortless to issue proclamations!**
>
> **How easily upweeded is this human life!**
>
> **By ruse of government I now am trapped.**
>
> **Reputation's all he seeks, I warrant you.**

LU QIU: Your head is wobbling on your shoulders. Go appeal to the
Prince—quick!

MURONG BAI: (*dejected*) I wanted to, but he's nowhere to be
found—who knows his whereabouts?

LU QIU: That's true.

(*aside*) The Prince has gone, that much I know. I can't
elaborate, even if I wanted to.

LORD DIAN: (*hurrying them*) Well, time to go. The Lord Protector
won't forgive us if we are late.

MURONG BAI: One more word, my lord, just one word.

(*to* LU QIU) Brother Lu, do me a big favor, please.

LU QIU: What is it?

MURONG BAI: My elder sister went to Xiuzhen Temple a couple of days ago, there to receive training in Daoism. She's no ordinary girl, for—

(*sings*)

> **A lovely, youthful maid is she, endowed**
> **As much with beauty as with charm.**
> **Her arguments persuasive, her discourse**
> **So learned and so reasonably framed,**
> **Debate's her forte—she's my only hope**
> **To be delivered from these ruthless laws!**

(*says*) Would you go to Xiuzhen Temple and ask her to petition to the Lord Protector as soon as possible?

LU QIU: Of course. Leave it to me. This is not only for you, but for all men in the world. It is too much indeed if for a game of tick-tack one should lose his life. I'm off now.

MURONG BAI: Thank you, good Brother Lu.

(*to* LORD DIAN) Come, my lord.

(*Exit* LORD DIAN *and the two* OFFICERS, *leading* MURONG BAI *away.*)

(*Light dims.*)

Scene 2: The Disguise

Location: Inside Chongxu Daoist Temple

(THE PRINCE *of Nanping and* MASTER QIU, *the Head Priest of the temple, are seen in a secret meeting.*)

THE PRINCE: Master Qiu, it has been announced that I was visiting North Tang on official business, and made Lord An Qilo Lord Protector of the land. But that is not the whole truth.

MASTER QIU: I crave enlightenment, Your Majesty.

THE PRINCE: My dear Head Priest, since times of old—

> (*sings*)
>
> **Wise sovereigns are known for statesmanship;**
>
> **With ease they govern, as if cooking smelt.**
>
> **Unbridled horses ne'er can run far:**
>
> **To tame them, all you need's a cracking whip.**
>
> **Alas, too milky-full of human kindnesses,**
>
> **I have let lie unused the biting laws**
>
> **Till now it's past the point of no return**
>
> **And quite adrift goes all morality.**
>
> **To start anew my mind is now made up:**

And he, Lord An, shall be my handy scourge.

(*says*) Therefore, I've imposed on Lord An the office to take aim at the guilty and strike home.

MASTER QIU: Yet Your Majesty can restore the laws whenever you please. Why leave it to someone else?

THE PRINCE: (*gesturing with a hand*) No. Our people—

(*sings*)

They are deceitful and unscrupulous;

But 'twas my fault to give them too-large scope.

To strike and gall them now would grievance cause;

I'd rather stand aloof, a spectator.

(*says*) Now, Lord An is a convenient pawn of ours. Since it was our fault to indulge the people all these years, we are responsible for the licentiousness permeating the land. If I gall the people with strict laws now, they'd find it unacceptable. (*pause*) Lord An is a man of firm abstinence and strictness; he should be able to mete out justice and caution the world on our behalf.

MASTER QIU: That is very thoughtful of Your Majesty.

THE PRINCE: There's a thing I need to trouble you with.

MASTER QIU: I'm at Your Majesty's service.

THE PRINCE: Supply me with your clothes, for I would be robed as a member of your order, the better to find out about

people's complaints—and to see if Lord An's measures can

reform our society.

MASTER QIU: Yes, Your Majesty. I'll go and have them ready

immediately. (*exit*)

THE PRINCE: (*in deep thought for a moment*) An Qilo, An Qilo,

now that you've been invested with our power, may you

prove our helping hand! We'll wait and see.

(*Light dims.*)

Scene 3: The Petition

Location: A conference room in the law court
(AN QILO *and* QUAN SHIKE *are discussing some business when a messenger enters, followed by* LORD DIAN *at some distance outside the hall.*)

MESSENGER: Your Honor, Lord Dian, Minister of Justice, craves your audience.

AN QILO: Let him come in.

(*Enter* LORD DIAN; *he pays respects.*)

AN QILO: What is it, Lord Dian?

LORD DIAN: My lord, your humble servant . . . your humble servant has come to know—if it is really your intention to execute Murong Bai at quarter to one tomorrow afternoon.

AN QILO: Humph! Have you not received the order? Why do you ask again?

LORD DIAN: Pardon me, Your Honor, I dare not disobey you. And yet . . . this order is too sudden, it does not have a precedent. I thought . . . maybe Your Honor would change your mind, and therefore . . . .

QUAN SHIKE: Indeed, my lord, and this gentleman is the only son of the deceased Magistrate Murong, an administrator of impeccable reputation and well liked by the people. Besides—

(*sings*)

> **The way to rule is magnanimity;**
>
> **From hist'ry learn, and show your people love.**
>
> **Since human life concerns heaven above,**
>
> **Better think thrice before one makes a move.**

AN QILO: (*turns to* QUAN SHIKE) My Lord Quan, we must never make a scarecrow of the law!

(*sings*)

> **My heavy trust's to curb debauchery;**
>
> **I heed not calumny nor petty fame.**
>
> **When has it been that power's come by chance?**
>
> **We censure one and hundreds will be warned.**

(*speaks, coldly*) My Lord Dian, the laws are not mere empty words, nor is my job a trifle.

(*resumes singing*)

> **'Tis unforgivable to knowingly**
>
> **Commit a crime. I'll never bend the law.**
>
> **Small doses hardly cure acute disease;**

Severe correction guarantees a moral world.

QUAN SHIKE: My lord—

(*sings*)

> Your life may be as clear as polished glass,
>
> Or like a piece of jade, unblemishèd.
>
> And yet if gods on you a trick do play,
>
> Would you not, then, for sensual pleasure fall?

(*speaks*) When that happens,

(*resumes singing*)

> You'd pull the law right down upon yourself.

(*speaks*) Ah, my lord—

(*resumes singing*)

> Best judge another's feelings by our own.

AN QILO: Why do you say this? This Murong Bai—

(*sings*)

> His crime does show he's no regard for law.
>
> What need is there for further argument?
>
> As matters stand he's forfeited his life.
>
> Your groundless supposition makes no sense.
>
> The day I'm caught in outlawed venery,

(*pauses, then unequivocally*)

> Let me be measured by the same decree.

(*speaks*) Murong Bai—he must be beheaded!

LORD QUAN: My lord . . .

AN QILO: (*gestures to* QUAN) No more of this.

(*Enter a* MESSENGER.)

MESSENGER: Your Honor, there's a girl outside who craves your audience. She says she's Murong Bai's sister.

AN QILO: Oh? He has a sister?

LORD DIAN: Yes, Your Honor. Ms. Murong is beautiful and wise. Since her parents passed away, she's said to be immersed in the study of Daoist scriptures. She is an advanced disciple now.

AN QILO: Well, call her in.

MESSENGER: Yes. (*exit*)

MURONG QING: (*offstage, sings*)

> **Across rough mountains and great shifting sands**
>
> **I've trudged since leaving convent door last night.**

(*Enter an* ATTENDANT, *leading* LU QIU, *with* MURONG QING *close behind.*)

(*resumes singing*)

> **Along the road stand blooming apricots**
>
> **And verdant willows; none appeal to me.**
>
> **The looming clouds forebode disaster here.**

To save my brother, my heart is all I've got.

MURONG QING and **LU QIU:** (*enter the hall and bow*) My respects to Your Honor.

AN QILO: Well, what's your will?

MURONG QING: I am a suitor to Your Honor.

AN QILO: What's your suit?

MURONG QING: It is a vice most unspeakable, for which I would not plead, but that I must.

AN QILO: Well, the matter?

MURONG QING: My younger brother, Murong Bai, is condemned to die.

AN QILO: Well, Murong Bai.

MURONG QING: Yes. I do beseech Your Honor to condemn the fault and not the man.

AN QILO: What? Condemn the fault, and not the actor of it? Nonsense! What kind of Lord Protector would I be, if I found faults clearly defined in the law and let loose the actor?

MURONG QING: O just but severe law! Poor my brother! (*takes one step backward, about to turn*)

LU QIU: (*whispers in haste to* MURONG QING) Don't give up like this. Entreat him! You're too cold. Even if you were just begging for a pin, you shouldn't be so cold. To him!

MURONG QING: (*steps forward*) Must he die?

AN QILO: No remedy.

MURONG QING: Yes, I do think you might pardon him. Heaven above takes pity on all living things. To obey the way of Nature is to comply with the will of the public.

AN QILO: I will not do it.

MURONG QING: But you can, if you would, can't you?

AN QILO: It's too late. He's sentenced.

LU QIU: (*whispers to* MURONG QING *again*) You're too cold.

MURONG QING: Too late? Why, no. True, the authority lies with Your Honor to pardon or to condemn, to give or to take, but mercy is Your Honor's most valuable grace. Had Your Honor been in my brother's place, you would have slipped like him, but he in yours would not have been so stern.

LU QIU: (*whispers to* MURONG QING *again*) Right, touch him; just like that.

AN QILO: (*gestures with his hand*) Your brother must face the law's penalty. You are wasting your words.

MURONG QING: I would to heaven I had your potency, and you were I. Should it then be thus? No, I would know the difference between the two.

AN QILO: It makes no difference. It is the law, not I, that condemns

your brother. Were he my brother, the sentence would still

stand. He must be executed tomorrow.

MURONG QING: Tomorrow? O, that's too sudden! Spare him!

He's so young. Your Honor—

(*sings*)

>How very dear does heaven cherish life!

>It always brings back spring to feed the earth.

>Compassion is the base of charity;

>Good deeds result from just a gentle thought.

>Watch out for ants, they say, e'en as you walk;

>And in thick woods no fire is allowed.

>Compassion leads to tolerance; a good

>Kings lead by virtue not by punishment.

>We should return to pristine purity:

>Enlighten all and give up none.

AN QILO: Why do you expound these views to me?

MURONG QING: Even when enforcing justice on behalf of heaven,

good my lord, one must not be so rash! Bethink you: Who

is it that has died for this offense? Many there are that

committed it!

LU QIU: (*whispers to* MURONG QING) Yes, well said!

AN QILO: The law has been, I do admit, merely a scarecrow—but it
was not abolished.

MURONG QING: Yet do show some pity.

AN QILO: I do show it most of all when I show justice; for then I
pity those I do not know. It is only right to mete out
rewards and punishments. Executing the villainous and
punishing the violent—only by such examples can future
crimes be prevented.

(*sings*)

Resolved to extirpate all maladies,

I'll never bend the law in any way.

It rests with me to foster good behavior;

I must restore our state to moral health.

(*speaks*) Your brother dies tomorrow.

MURONG QING: O, it is excellent to have a giant's strength, my
lord, but it is tyrannous to abuse it. My lord—

(*sings*)

Man's life's an evanescent dream, the moon

Reflected in the sea, a mirrored bud.

Sage sovereigns crave no worldly fame, but their

Upright example lets them rule with ease.

A middle course can rectify the world;

Excessive measures ruin heaven's work.

AN QILO: (*as if touched*) Well! This . . .

(*sings an aside*)

> **As sudden peals of thunder in the spring**
>
> **Arouse the torpid hibernating life,**
>
> **So, too, as if awakened from a dream,**
>
> **With more attention will I listen now.**

LU QIU: (*aside*) Looks like the Lord Protector will soon relent . . .

QUAN SHIKE: (*aside*) May she win Lord An!

MURONG QING: All things on earth are created differently; we
must not weigh others by our own scales.

(*sings*)

> **All creatures are endowed with divers nature.**
>
> **How can we sit in reckless judgment then?**
>
> **A sparrow never thinks of flying south;**
>
> **A summer insect knows not winter ice;**
>
> **Officials get away with setting fire,**
>
> **While commoners must leave their lamps unlit.**
>
> **Go to your bosom—ask your heart if it**
>
> **Too knows a fault that's like my brother's fault.**

(*speaks*) If you, my lord, following your natural bent, have
entertained the same guilty thought, please spare my

brother's life.

AN QILO: (*to all*) Well, I will consider this case. You may leave now.

(*to* MURONG QING) Come again tomorrow.

MURONG QING: (*slightly gladdened*) Ah, thank you, my lord. May Your Honor's vast happiness be as boundless as the heaven!

QUAN SHIKE and **LORD DIAN:** We take our leave.

(*Exeunt.*)

AN QILO: (*forcing a smile*) My vast happiness? What's this? I've always curbed my desire and abided by the law; never once have I done anything improper. And yet, today, I'm quite, quite subdued—

(*sings*)

This maid—so full of grace, her ringing voice so
clear,

Her beauty peerless—is a nonpareil.

This maid—so widely read and to the point,

Her every word a gem—is eloquent.

Poor me—so fascinated, tossed about,

I can't control my own emotions wild.

Poor me—sitting or standing, I'm besotted;

Uneasy, restless, I can't make up my mind.

The sight, the scene—so unforgettable!

To pardon or to kill? I must deliberate.

(AN QILO *shakes his head, looking rather disturbed.*)

(*Light dims.*)

Scene 4: A Secret Visit

Location: A prison

(*Enter* LORD DIAN, *a secret missive in his hand, and* THE PRINCE *disguised as a Daoist priest.*)

LORD DIAN: So, Master Wen, it appears that His Majesty (*pointing to the missive*) has arranged for you to inspect the prison?

THE PRINCE: Well, my lord, that's a bit overstated. His Majesty simply wants me to pray for blessings and dispel any inauspiciousness, while enlightening by the way those condemned to death. . . . Well, have there been any special cases lately?

LORD DIAN: Indeed there is one. Murong Bai, the son of the late Magistrate Murong, for making his fiancée pregnant, has been sentenced to death by the Lord Protector. He is soon to be executed.

THE PRINCE: Oh? Is that so? Let me talk with young Master Murong.

LORD DIAN: Yes, this way please.

(LORD DIAN *leads the Prince to* MURONG BAI's *cell.*)

(*calls to the jailor*) Open up the cell!

(*The jailor opens it.*)

LORD DIAN: Master Murong, this is Master Wen, a Daoist priest, who would like to talk to you.

MURONG BAI: (*listless*) What's there to talk about? Unless it's about the Lord Protector's pardon!

(THE PRINCE *makes a gesture, and* LORD DIAN *nods and exits.*)

THE PRINCE: So you eagerly hope for a pardon?

MURONG BAI: The miserable have no other choice but hope. Alas!

THE PRINCE: You must have courage and be ready for death. Both death and life shall then be easier to bear. You must realize—

(*sings*)

> **The whole wide world is but a mustard seed;**
> **'Tis foolish with the feverish world to vie.**
> **Why waste one's life in search of mere illusion?**
> **Time slips away as fame and gain we crave.**
> **Forgetting essences, we lose ourselves.**
> **Willy-nilly, we come to the same ends.**
> **Thus death is life and life, death. Erase**
> **Distinctions, and heaven's equals we become.**

(*speaks*) Therefore, to understand the great Way that transcends life and death is something for you to ponder at this moment.

MURONG BAI: Ah! I'm much bound to you for enlightening me. But life and death is such a serious matter—

(*sings*)

> **Much easier it's said than trusted home!**
>
> **Yet heed I will for what it's worth.**
>
> **E'en more mysterious is death than life.**
>
> **Perplexed, in this shall I believe or no?**

THE PRINCE: (*produces a copy of* The Classic of Supreme Peace *to* MURONG BAI, *sings*)

> **To see through life and death, no easy task,**
>
> **These sheets may render you some food for thought.**
>
> **Peruse the subtle words and weigh their drift;**
>
> **No need to be concerned with gain and loss.**

(*speaks*) Study this volume of *The Classic of Supreme Peace* and meditate on it. I will come again to visit you. Take care of yourself.

MURONG BAI: Much obliged, Master priest.

(*They fold their hands and bid each other farewell.* THE PRINCE *steps out of the cell and nods to the jailor to lock the door.*)

THE PRINCE: This is a bit odd . . .

(*He meets* LU QIU *at the door.*)

LU QIU: Why, Master priest, please stay awhile.

(*sizing him up*) You're not from around here, are you?

THE PRINCE: Well, I just arrived from the north. I heard there is a Daoist service here to exorcise the evil . . .

LU QIU: That's right. So you've come from the north. What news, Monk, of our Prince?

THE PRINCE: I know none. Can you tell me any?

LU QIU: Some say he's with the Prince of East Hua; others say he is in North Tang. But where is he, do you think?

THE PRINCE: I don't know. Wherever he is, I can only wish him well.

LU QIU: Ha! It was a fantastical trick of him to steal from the state and usurp the beggary he was never born to. (*sarcastically*) Lord An substitutes well in his absence; he enforces the law strictly . . .

THE PRINCE: That's as it should be.

LU QIU: Yet, a little more lenity to lechery would do him no harm. Something too harsh that way.

THE PRINCE: It is too general a vice, and severity must cure it.

LU QIU: True, but, Monk, "Appetite for food and sex is basic to human nature"; it is impossible to completely prohibit it, unless eating and drinking are put down also! (*lowers his voice*) Why, what a ruthless person is he to take the life of a man simply for the rebellion of a codpiece! (*raising his voice*) Would that the Prince were back! How I wish he were back! (*looks around, lowers his voice again*) This queer Lord Protector will surely deplete the state of its population. Would the Prince that's absent have done this?

THE PRINCE: What do you say?

LU QIU: Our beloved Prince, he-he! (*lowers his voice*) is an expert in the sport; he knew the service. That's why (*loudly*) he's so kind-hearted.

THE PRINCE: I never heard the prince charged with womanizing. He was not inclined that way.

LU QIU: Ha! My priest, you're deceived. The Prince (*lowers his voice*) would have dark deeds darkly answered. You wouldn't know how many "bosom" friends he has in the House of Pleasant Spring! Just two months ago, we went to a brothel together. (*loudly*) The Prince knew that I got Spring Charm with child, and he said nothing.

THE PRINCE: Impossible!

LU QIU: Impossible? Hmm, nothing is impossible in this world. Let me tell you, the Prince would be drunk too. He's even founded a private Wine Party.

THE PRINCE: You are either mistaken, or maliciously slandering. As far as I know, our Prince is a wise ruler.

LU QIU: Come, sir, I know what I know.

THE PRINCE: Is that so? May I know your name, young master?

LU QIU: My name is Lu Qiu, well known to the Prince.

THE PRINCE: Good. If I live to report you to him, he shall certainly remember you.

LU QIU: Ha ha! Is this a threat? I fear you not. Go ahead and make your report. Say that Lu Qiu said so. Farewell, I'm on my way to visit some friends. (*exit*)

THE PRINCE: (*shaking his head and forcing a smile*) Even a king cannot tie the gall up in the slanderous tongue!

[Chorus]

> **Endowed with pow'r to frighten people's souls,**
>
> **Yet powerless to censor roguish smears:**
>
> **It's nice to bathe in springtime's gentle balm,**
>
> **But frosty words in June pour ice on men!**

(*Light dims.*)

Scene 5: The Blackmail

Location: the conference room of the court

(AN QILO *is seen pacing in meditation.*)

AN QILO: (*sings*)

> **My brows knitted, I'm torturing myself,**
>
> **Sleepless the whole night, as in a trance.**
>
> **Many a pretty woman have I seen,**
>
> **And yet I fell for her upon first sight.**
>
> **To none can I reveal my lustful stirrings;**
>
> **Like rain in spring they simply do not stop.**
>
> **The watchman's drums announce the break of day,**
>
> (*resolved*)
>
> **I'll boldly go ahead, no turning back!**

(*speaks*) I've always appeared prim and sanctimonious, but now I couldn't care less about that. . . .

(*Enter a court* ATTENDANT.)

ATTENDANT: My lord, one Murong Qing desires access to you.

AN QILO: Bring her in.

ATTENDANT: Yes. (*exit*)

(MURONG QING *enters and does obeisance to* AN QILO,
who nods his head slightly in return.)

MURONG QING: Your Honor, I am come to know your pleasure.

AN QILO: That you might know my pleasure, and be willing to
cooperate, would much more please me. Your brother—
cannot live.

MURONG QING: (*after a slight pause, decides to give up*) Well,
then. May Your Honor's vast happiness be as boundless as
the heaven! (*takes a step backward, about to leave*)

AN QILO: Yet may he live awhile, or even longer. It all depends—

MURONG QING: (*her hope rekindled*) On you?

AN QILO: No. On *you.*

MURONG QING: Oh?

AN QILO: Let's put it this way. Your brother has committed an
abominable crime, unworthy of pardon—and like a killer
must pay with his life.

MURONG QING: Yet, Your Honor, my brother's offense was one
of consensual love and did not harm anyone. How can it be
compared to homicide?

AN QILO: Is that so? Well, then, let me ask you this: Suppose—let's
just suppose—there's a choice, what would you do?—Let
your brother be immediately executed according to the just

law, or, to save him, lay down the treasure of your body

and enjoy the sweetness of union?

MURONG QING: Your Honor, I would rather endure the harshest

tortures than betray my conscience.

AN QILO: I am not concerned about your conscience.

MURONG QING: You mean—

AN QILO: I, now the voice of the recorded law, pronounce a

sentence on your brother's life. Might there not be a mercy

in sin to save his life?

MURONG QING: Certainly, it is no sin at all, but mercy. If you

show this charity, I will make it my morning and evening

prayer with burning incense to the Revered God of Triple

Purity, to keep Your Honor.

AN QILO: Fie! You do not understand me. Hear me again: Suppose

there were one who could save your brother — on the

condition that you sleep with him; would you consent to do

it?

MURONG QING: My lord, I would rather die than defile my Daoist

practice of purity.

AN QILO: Were you not then as cruel as the law—to watch your

brother lose his life?

MURONG QING: Your Honor, lawful mercy comes from human

nature; it is not at all akin to foul redemption!

AN QILO: Just now you argued vehemently that your brother's

offense was one of consensual love and nothing foul?

MURONG QING: Ah, to save his life, I had to excuse him. Pardon

me, my lord, my cowardliness in speaking not what I mean.

AN QILO: Now that you've admitted your frailty, you might as well

leave off your pretense.

MURONG QING: I don't follow you . . . . What do you mean, my

lord?

AN QILO: Right. (*gives her a meaningful look*) Now listen carefully:

(*sings*)

> **I'm overwhelmed by you, do you not see?**

> **Deep-rooted lovesickness bear I for you.**

MURONG QING: (*shocked*) Ah? My lord, you—

(*sings*)

> **You wag your tongue so freely it's absurd!**

> **Such joking words befit a ruler not.**

AN QILO: (*sings*)

> **Those words I spoke from th' bottom of my heart:**

> **A one-night tryst can save a criminal.**

MURONG QING: (*sings*)

> **The law of purity of nature we**

Must keep. Illicit sex is shame indeed.

AN QILO: (*sings*)

If you intend to save your brother's life,

One coupling will unload your worries all.

MURONG QING: (*sings*)

Such a scheming, dirty mind's unheard of!

I'll make no deal with one of no integrity.

(*speaks*) Ha! An Qilo, so you're an insidious hypocrite!

Sign me a present pardon for my brother, or I'll expose you

to the world!

AN QILO: (*snickering*) Humph! Go ahead and expose me! But who

will believe you? My unsoiled name and high place in the

state will turn your charges into calumny and land you in

prison! Now, stop teasing me with your coyness, but just

yield to my will. Or—by my present thought, your brother

must not only die, but suffer lingering death. Humph!

Answer me tomorrow.

(*He exits in anger.*)

MURONG QING: O Heaven! To whom can I complain? Who would

believe me? O despicable, damnable An Qilo!

(*sings*)

A high official, he intimidates,

And takes advantage of my helplessness.

A hypocrite, he's hoodwinked everyone:

Who could have known he's utterly depraved?

What could have driven him such dirty thoughts

To entertain? There is no cause at all.

(MURONG QING *paces back and forth, now bending her head to look at herself, now stopping in reverie.*)

[Chorus]

Perhaps the unadorned can more seduce?

A maiden pure more winsome than a flirt?

Or have you, tactless in the use of words,

This trouble courted, signals wrongly sent?

MURONG QING: (*angry*) What does my plain dress have to do with love? And did I say anything amorously suggestive in the slightest? It is totally unthinkable that it should come to this. . . .

(*sings*)

My honor, my repute, I cannot trash.

Yet will he lightly let me off the hook?

O how I hate deceitful hypocrites!

And now I'm at the end of my tether.

(*seems to stare into the distance, sunk in thought*)

[Chorus]

Alas, unhappy day! One sorrow heaped

Upon another—heavy desolation!

What course to take? For long I hesitate,

Mixed feelings in my mind do roil.

MURONG QING: (*her mind made up*) Well! More than our life is our honor. I'll go see my brother now and tell him my decision.

(*Light dims.*)

(*Intermission*)

Scene 6: The Advice

Locations: Area A: MURONG BAI's prison cell; Area B: a side-room in the prison; Area C: FU QIAOYIN's country house

(*Area A:* MURONG BAI's *prison cell*)

(THE PRINCE, *disguised as a Daoist pirest, is seen debating the Way with* MURONG BAI)

THE PRINCE: . . . therefore, in the Way, there is no desire nor

craving.

MURONG BAI: I humbly thank you for pointing out the way.

(*Enter* LORD DIAN, *leading* MURONG QING.)

LORD DIAN: Master Wen, this is young Master Murong's sister.

MURONG QING: (*greets him*) Master, please allow me to talk with

my brother in private.

THE PRINCE: (*returns the bow*) Please do.

(THE PRINCE *and* LORD DIAN *walk a few steps upstage.*)

THE PRINCE: Lord Dian, please bring me to hear them speak,

where I may be concealed.

LORD DIAN: This way please.

(*Exeunt.*)

MURONG BAI: Now, sister, what's the comfort?

MURONG QING: Alas, my dear brother, the Lord Protector, having affairs with the Jade Emperor, intends you for his swift ambassador to Heaven.

MURONG BAI: (*suspicious*) Meaning—?

MURONG QING: Meaning—to execute you.

MURONG BAI: (*downhearted*) Ah . . .

MURONG QING: Unless . . .

MURONG BAI: (*eyes suddenly quickening, holds his sister's hands*) Unless what?

MURONG QING: Alas, my dear brother—

(*sings*)

>Together, you and I, so many days from morn to
>   night,
>Have we talked over art or books by the window.
>I only wish you'd follow father's foot-
>Steps, find a match, enjoy the bliss of marriage.
>Alas, we're fortune's fools, and have no luck.
>Prosperity, a dream, does not last long.
>The Lord Protector—he's a shameless beast in
>   human dress.
>Your sister cannot ope her mouth and speak.

**I have no choice but weep and bid you sad
good-bye,
Henceforth to seek the Way among the clouds.**

MURONG BAI: Dear sister, don't keep me guessing! You can be
honest with your brother. This Lord Protector is a man of
complete integrity; how can he be a beast in human dress?

MURONG QING: (*agitated*) He a man of complete integrity? Right,
a complete villain is he! All of us, including the Prince,
have been deceived in him. He would pardon you, but only
under a most preposterous, shameless condition.

MURONG BAI: Oh? What condition?

MURONG QING: If I agree to this condition, even if it could save
your life, you'd be so grieved as to wish to die, for life
imprisonment of conscience is a punishment more cruel
than decapitation. As for me—I certainly could not drag out
this ignoble life.

MURONG BAI: What exactly is the condition? Let me know the
point.

MURONG QING: If I would—yield him my virginity, you might
live.

MURONG BAI: O heaven! It cannot be.

MURONG QING: Yes, that is the truth. Were it but my life, I'd throw it down for you. My dear brother, reputation is the most important thing in life. Some things one ought to do, and some things one mustn't do. To preserve life by adultery is utterly unacceptable!

MURONG BAI: Ah, my dear sister!

MURONG QING: When the Prince returns, I will surely enter charges on your behalf.

MURONG BAI: Dear sister!

MURONG QING: My brother!

(*They hold each other's hands, sobbing.*)

MURONG BAI: (*suddenly hit by an idea*) Dear sister, has the Lord Protector passions in him that can make him flout the law when enforcing it? Surely then—

MURONG QING: What then, my brother?

MURONG BAI: Dear sister, if the Lord Protector has made this proposition, doesn't it mean that fornication is nothing very serious?

MURONG QING: Dear brother, you . . .

MURONG BAI: Alas, sweet sister—

(*sings*)

> **To die, and go we know not where, but sure**
> **To stand naked before the Mirror of Sins.**

> In smoky, foggy fields of yellow sand
>
> The soul would roam, get lost in vast expanse.

MURONG QING: What exactly do you want to say?

MURONG BAI: Dear sister—

(resumes singing)

> The soul in pieces, no memory remains;
>
> The dead forever severed from the living.
>
> Their lot? Bone-chilling ice or mound of knives
>
> Sharp-pointed, burning posts of brass, or iron
>
> beds—
>
> Unending torture, most unspeakable!
>
> A loathèd life is paradise to peaceful death.

MURONG QING: What? What do you mean?

MURONG BAI: Sweet sister, let me live! For saving me, your
sacrifice cannot be sin, but a noble deed!

MURONG QING: O you beast! To say what you have said! You,
you . . .

(sings)

> In vain have you pursued the way of learning—
>
> Such filthy words to utter, turning all
>
> To ruin! What foolish thoughts you entertain!
>
> You'd swallow insults just to live, you lecher!

(*speaks*) No brother of mine now, forget the wishful

thinking that I would plead for you!

(*resumes singing*)

It's shameful lechery that's cost your life,

A fitting punishment you well deserve.

MURONG BAI: Do hear me, sweet sister . . .

MURONG QING: O, fie! No more of this! Your sin's not accidental;

you're simply shameless! Die, perish! Mercy to you would

prove itself a bawd!

MURONG BAI: Oh, sweet sister, do hear me . . .

(*Enter* THE PRINCE)

THE PRINCE: I have overheard your conversation.

(*to* MURONG QING) On this matter, I have an idea that

you might want to consider.

MURONG QING: Oh? Please instruct me.

THE PRINCE: Come, let's talk outside.

(*to* MURONG BAI) You must focus on the Daoist scripture.

Do not indulge in fallible hopes.

(MURONG BAI *nods in silence.*)

(THE PRINCE *and* MURONG QING *walk out of the cell*

and turn into the side-room.)

(Area B: A side-room in the prison)

THE PRINCE: You, Madame, are as good as you're fair. The
heaven will surely protect you. What will you do now?

MURONG QING: Master priest, I'm going to that beast in human
form and set his mind at rest. When the Prince returns I'll
appeal to him.

THE PRINCE: That is well and good. Yet, Lord An Qilo will
certainly avoid your accusation, saying that it's nothing but
your revengeful slander. Thus not only will your brother
wrongfully die and your reputation be soiled, but Lord An
Qilo may even be further promoted.

MURONG QING: Well . . .

THE PRINCE: I like to roam about and defend people against
injustice. If you think me trustworthy, I think I have a
clever idea that could not only save your brother and keep
your honor, but also help a poor wronged lady.

MURONG QING: Well, let me hear it. As long as it's something I
can do with a clear conscience, I'll do it.

THE PRINCE: Good. Have you heard of General Fu, who
miscarried at sea several years ago?

MURONG QING: Yes. General Fu was a very high official who had
served the state with distinction.

THE PRINCE: His younger sister was engaged to Lord An. Just before the marriage, General Fu perished at the sea, along with the marriage dowry of his sister. Shortly afterwards, Lord An broke off the engagement, citing as excuse discoveries of dishonor in the lady.

MURONG QING: Ha! Can this be so?

THE PRINCE: Yes. And to this day the innocent lady has not been able to free herself from the grief . . . .

(*Area C:* FU QIAOYIN *is seen playing a zither, demonstrating all sorts of postures*)

> [Chorus]
>> **The music's stopped, the song is done.**
>>
>> **How chilly, mournful are the livelong days!**
>>
>> **Disaster-hit, I've lost my chief support;**
>>
>> **My make-up I remove with trickling tears.**

FU QIAOYIN: (*continues the song*)

>> **To the lute alone can I my secret tell,**
>>
>> **For fear my passion may be ridiculed.**
>>
>> **No matter how reluctant, full of gall,**
>>
>> **I can't forget that traitor's tenderness.**
>>
>> **This lovesickness of mine—where can I send?**

I trust it to flow'rs wherever they're blown.

(*Light dims on Area C.*)

MURONG QING: But that doesn't help, does it?

THE PRINCE: No. Yet Lady Fu, extremely romantic, just cannot forget Lord An. Go you to Lord An and agree to his request, but make three conditions: First, that your stay may not be too long; second, that the place be secret; third, that the time be dark midnight. I shall persuade Lady Fu to go in your stead. By this is your brother saved, your honor untainted, and, when the Prince returns to uphold justice, it will be to Lady Fu's advantage. After all, they were legally engaged.

MURONG QING: (*overjoyed and most grateful*) How wonderful! I thank you. What an excellent idea! Fare you well.

THE PRINCE: Rest assured. I will take care of everything.

(THE PRINCE *nods, smiling; then solicitously he accompanies* MURONG QING *to the door and watches her leave.*)

(*Light dims.*)

Scene 7: The Prisoner Delivered

Location: the Prison

(XIANG YU's *cell*)

XIANG YU: Hey! There's risk in every walk of life. Even a mustard seed may fall into a needle's eye. A little carelessness on my part and I was nabbed. But here in the prison, ha ha! I am as well familiar as I was in our house. They say, "In the mountain the hunter sees nothing but beasts, and the herb farmer nothing but herbs." I look around and see nothing but old customers. There, and there, and there, (*pointing to the audience at will*) Manager Li, Officer Zhang, Song "the merciless official," Young Master Ke . . . Well, well, well, everybody is here . . . not a single one missing . . .

(*Enter* LORD DIAN *with the cell* ATTENDANT; *he signals the attendant to open the cell door to let* XIANG YU *out.*)

LORD DIAN: Hey, Sirrah, can you cut off a man's head?

XIANG YU: Ha! If the man be a villain, sure! But if it belongs to an elder or a woman or a child, I should yield my seat to them instead of cutting off their heads!

LORD DIAN: Come, leave off your quips. The Lord Protector has ordered the execution of Murong Bai tomorrow. It is not the right season and our executioner lacks an assistant. If you would change your profession, you'd be spared hard labor; if not, you'll serve twenty years' time, for you have been a bawd.

XIANG YU: My lord, I'd rather be a hangman than serve twenty years in this prison.

LORD DIAN: All right. Go call the executioner.

(*Exit the* ATTENDANT. *Enter* HE BAOSHENG, *the executioner.*)

HE BAOSHENG: Do you call, sir?

LORD DIAN: Sirrah, this fellow here shall follow you from now on. Instruct him. He has been a bawd, nothing to compare with you.

HE BAOSHENG: What? A bawd? Your honor, "Goats and wolves are no relatives; mice and cats do not marry each other." He's not of my class, he'll be a disgrace to our craft!

XIANG YU: (*rushing to speak*) Hey, dear brother, don't get me wrong. I manned a bar. A bartender who mixes drinks. Mixing drinks is also a demanding craft. (*to the audience*) You do agree, don't you?

LORD DIAN: (*to* HE BAOSHENG) Put up with him, for we can't find anyone suitable. Go, get ready.

XIANG YU: (*rushes to* HE BAOSHENG, *palsy-walsy*) Big brother, do teach me the tricks of the head-cutting craft. I desire to learn. I'll remember your kindness and, when you need my service someday, you'll find me quick and eager. I'll make sure you don't suffer much. . . .

(*Exeunt as* XIANG YU *butters up* HE BAOSHENG.)

LORD DIAN: Alas, Murong Bai . . . (*shakes his head*)

(*Enter* THE PRINCE.)

THE PRINCE: Have you no countermand for young Master Murong yet?

LORD DIAN: None. (*suspicious*) Will there be one, do you think?

THE PRINCE: Should be coming soon.

(*rapid knocking within*)

THE PRINCE: (*glowing with joy*) It's here, it's here.

(*Enter a* MESSENGER, *a piece of paper in hand.*)

MESSENGER: My lord, the Lord Protector has sent this express command.

(*He hands the paper and exits.* LORD DIAN *reads the command.*)

THE PRINCE: (*aside*) This is his pardon, purchased by such sin for which the pardoner himself is in.

(LORD DIAN *looks surprised.*)

THE PRINCE: What's the matter?

LORD DIAN: This is an unusual act by the Lord Protector. It is not a pardon.

THE PRINCE: Oh? What does it say?

LORD DIAN: Now listen—(*reads the letter*) "In any case, execute Murong Bai at three o'clock. By quarter past five have his head sent to me. Let this be duly performed." It's now a quarter to three already . . . .

THE PRINCE: This is truly unexpected! (*takes over the letter and gives it a look-through*) Your Honor, we must find a way to preserve him.

LORD DIAN: Well . . . I dare not.

THE PRINCE: (*thinks for a moment, then produces the royal jade seal*) Your Honor, come take a look at this.

LORD DIAN: Ah! The royal seal! This . . . you are . . . ?

THE PRINCE: Hush! (*looks around*) Heaven's secrets must not be revealed!

LORD DIAN: Yes, yes, Your Majesty. (*about to kneel down*)

THE PRINCE: (*preventing him*) No need. (*putting away the seal*) My Lord Dian, how shall we proceed now?

LORD DIAN: Well . . .

(*The two men are lost in thought.*)

[Chorus]

An obstacle out of the blue indeed!

They ponder long, a surefire way to find,

With prudence contemplating every move,

Till suddenly they hit upon a thought.

LORD DIAN: (*hit by an idea*) Ah, yes, half an hour ago, here in the

prison died a bandit, a man of young Master Murong's age.

With a few tricks, we might satisfy the Lord Protector with

him.

THE PRINCE: (*pleasantly surprised*) O, this is providence! Do it

then. Be quick!

LORD DIAN: Yes.

THE PRINCE: Wait! You also need to hide Murong Bai somewhere.

In a couple of days things will become clear. Quick!

LORD DIAN: Yes. (*Exit.*)

(*After some pondering,* THE PRINCE *scribbles something*

and seals it.)

(*Enter* MURONG QING *led by an* ATTENDANT, *who then*

leaves.)

MURONG QING: (*pays respects*) Sir Priest, has my brother's pardon arrived?

THE PRINCE: (*gets up and returns the bow*) Madam, Lord An's just ordered his release—

MURONG QING: (*elated*) Really?

THE PRINCE: Really. From this world, for good.—He has been executed.

MURONG QING: (*incredulous*) Huh? But, Lady Fu has come back from the tryst. How could this be?

THE PRINCE: Unfortunately it is so.

MURONG QING: (*indignant*) O my poor brother! O damnable An Qilo!

(*sings*)

>How hateful O this foxy, tricky schemer,
>
>Pulling the wool o'er everybody's eyes!
>
>His vow still rings so clearly in my ear,
>
>Yet he has torn from me my flesh and blood.
>
>Treacherous thief more brutal than a wolf,
>
>He's compelled me to suffer mute and dumb.
>
>My heart is cleft, my tears I can't hold back.
>
>Beyond endurance, this wrong I will redress!

(*Covering her face, she wails bitterly.*)

THE PRINCE: (*calmly*) There, there, dry your eyes. Listen to me.

According to reliable information, the Prince returns

tomorrow. Come! (*steps forward to hold* MURONG

QING's *hand, then turns around to pick up the letter on the*

table) Take this letter to Priest Qiu, head of Chongxu

Daoist Temple. Say that I desire him to bring you and Lady

Fu, tomorrow afternoon at one o'clock, to the city gate, to

protest injustice to the Prince on his return. The rest I'll

take care of.

MURONG QING: (*suspicious; wipes tears*) Yes, Sir Priest.

THE PRINCE: (*firmly*) The Prince will give you the justice you

deserve.

(*patting* MURONG QING *on her shoulder, gently*) Believe

me. Rest assured!

MURONG QING: I thank you, Sir Priest. (*exit*)

THE PRINCE: (*sings*)

> **A king does well with gentleness to govern;**
>
> **In all sincerity he cares for all.**
>
> **The people's interest always kept in mind,**
>
> **He guarantees a world that's trouble-free.**
>
> **In sentencing he is adaptable;**
>
> **He weighs with care before he judgment makes.**
>
> **Securing private gain by crafty means**

Is what he hates; deceit he won't allow.

To bring back justice can brook no delay.

Just wait and see—I'll forge a stratagem to trap the fox!

(*Light dims.*)

Scene 8: Measure, Measure!

Location: The city gate

AN QILO: (*sings*)

> An eminent member of the highest rank,
>
> I was a man of peerless probity.
>
> One false step's landed me in desperate straits:
>
> Not keeping faith, now I deserve to die.
>
> Whatever scheme I use to cheat the world,
>
> Eventually the truth will be exposed.
>
> In utter stupefaction is my mind;
>
> How shamefully do I regret it all!

(*speaks*) O, may this maiden's tender shame or fear of my authority prevent her from proclaiming it. . . . Alas, he should have lived, but that his riotous youth might not swallow the shame in the times to come. . . . Alas, what has become of me? Will nothing go right once we have forgotten our grace? O heavens!

(*Enter* QUAN SHIKE *and other dignitaries.*)

QUAN SHIKE, ETC.: Your Honor!

AN QILO: Ah, my lords!

(They greet each other and then line up to welcome THE PRINCE. *Crowds of citizens,* LU QIU *among them, also line up along the street, shouting for joy.)*

AN QILO: My Lord Quan, didn't His Majesty send word a couple of days ago that he was still in West Qi and could not return any time soon?

QUAN SHIKE: Indeed. The news we've received these days is all at odds. I, too, am clueless about this mystery.

AN QILO: I wonder why his messages contradict each other. And this hand-written decree especially instructs that we allow citizens to petition at the city gate—what do you think this means?

QUAN SHIKE: Your Honor, it would be circumspect for us to follow his instruction. Yesterday, therefore, I had it proclaimed all over with posters and loud beating of the gong.

(Enter a MESSENGER.*)*

MESSENGER: *(announces)* His Majesty the Prince of Nanping.

THE PRINCE: *(offstage, sings)*

It's been a grueling journey all the way,

(THE PRINCE *hurries in on horseback.*)

(*resumes singing*)

To fullest speed I spurred my flying horse.

A plan I have to clean up filthy dirt;

The time is now that we reform the state.

AN QILO, QUAN SHIKE, ETC.: (*stepping forward*) Happy return

to Your Royal Majesty!

THE PRINCE: (*dismounts; to* AN QILO *and* QUAN SHIKE) Thank

you both. We have heard on the way back much goodness

of your impartial justice. You are indeed our best assistants

worthy of commendation.

AN QILO and **QUAN SHIKE:** Your Majesty over-praises us.

AN QILO: Your humble servant has merely done his duty in loyalty.

THE PRINCE: Ha ha! You're too modest!

(*Enter* PRIEST QIU *and* MURONG QING.)

PRIEST QIU: Now is the time; go.

MURONG QING: (*steps forward, kneels down*) Justice, Your

Majesty! Give me justice, justice, justice, justice!

THE PRINCE: Oh? What's your wrong? Lord An is here, he shall

give you justice. Relate your wrongs to him.

MURONG QING: O royal Prince, you bid me seek redemption of

the devil. Hear me yourself, I beg of you!

AN QILO: My lord, her wits are not firm. She has been a suitor to me for her brother cut off by course of justice.

MURONG QING: (*suddenly stands up*) By course of justice! By

course of justice?

AN QILO: She will chop and change, and speak most strangely.

MURONG QING: O Your Majesty, my charge may seem strange,

but it is not.

(*pointing at* AN QILO) He—

(*sings*)

An Qilo, you hypocrite! Deceiver!

You cheat and use your place for private gain.

Premeditated murder and deflow'ring

A virgin—these are despicable crimes!

THE PRINCE: Well, strange indeed.

Away with her! She is obviously mentally deranged.

(*Two* ATTENDANTS *step forward.*)

MURONG QING: No, my lord—

(*resumes singing*)

Although it seems a drama most absurd,

There's nothing but the truth in what I say.

(*The Prince motions to the* ATTENDANTS *to draw back.*)

MURONG QING: Some sordid rogues are always courteous; some

archvillains dressed impeccably. O Your Majesty—

(*sings*)

This world is full of contradictions, and

It's hard to penetrate the heart of man.

A treacherous traitor oft prudent seems;

In visage serious, but faint of heart.

Unbiased and with care should we observe,

To find the truth with perspicacity.

THE PRINCE: (*to* AN QILO *and* QUAN SHIKE) Her words are too coherent to have come from a mad person—even though we believe she *is* mad.

(*to the* ATTENDANTS) Go bring two chairs.

(*Chairs are placed.* THE PRINCE *and* AN QILO *take seats.*)

(*to* MURONG QING) Now, what would you say?

MURONG QING: I am the elder sister of Murong Bai, condemned upon the act of fornication to lose his head. I was then a novice at Xiuzhen Daoist Temple. My brother sent one Master Lu Qiu to bring me the message—

LU QIU: (*steps forward to interrupt*) That's me, Your Majesty. I then escorted the lady to plead with Lord An for her brother's pardon.

MURONG QING: Indeed.

THE PRINCE: (*to* LU QIU) You were not bid to speak.

LU QIU: Nor wished to hold my peace.

THE PRINCE: Silence! When it's your turn to testify, pray heaven
you then be perfect.

LU QIU: I warrant Your Majesty.

THE PRINCE: Warrant? Take heed you perjure not.

(*to* MURONG QING) Proceed.

MURONG QING: I Went to this pernicious caitiff Lord Protector . . .

THE PRINCE: (*to* AN QILO) That's madly spoken again.

MURONG QING: In short, after my repeated pleading, (*pointing to*
AN QILO) this man here—he made a shameless demand—

THE PRINCE: Oh? What demand?

MURONG QING: Your Majesty, he—he—would not, unless I gave
him my chastity, release my brother. And after much debate,
my sisterly love prevailed against my honor. I yielded to
him. But, his lust satisfied, he immediately ordered the
execution of my brother.

THE PRINCE: Ridiculous! Is this some freakish tale from old? This
is most likely!

MURONG QING: Your Majesty, I dare not lie. This is true and true!

THE PRINCE: You are either mad or suborned against him. Do you
know the consequence of libeling a high-ranking court

official? Lord An's impeccable integrity is there for all to
see. If he had, as you charge, committed fornication, he
would have weighed your brother by himself, and pardoned
him.

Say, who has set you on to lodge such preposterous
complaints? Tell us the truth!

MURONG QING: If Your Majesty does not believe, what more can
I say? I can only crave Heaven's mercy! (*starts to leave*)

THE PRINCE: Just a minute! Shall we thus permit a scandalous
breath to fall on him so near to us? An officer! Detain her.

(*Two* OFFICERS *come up to arrest* MURONG QING.)

This must be a practice. Say, who sent you here?

MURONG QING: One Master Wen, a Daoist priest. I wish he were
here.

THE PRINCE: To prison with her until further notice.

(*Exit* MURONG QING *under guard of two* OFFICERS.)

A goodly Daoist priest! Humph, who knows this Priest
Wen?

LU QIU: Your Majesty, I know him. He's a meddling priest. Just
two days ago I met him at the prison gate, and he loudly
criticized you. Had he been a layman, I would have boxed
him in the ear.

THE PRINCE: Criticize me? How dare he! Go, bring him here.

(*Exit two* OFFICERS.)

MASTER QIU: Your Majesty, I know something about this. In fact, this woman here should not have accused Lord An, for she is unsoiled; Lord An never touched her. This I can prove.

THE PRINCE: Oh? This is interesting. Prove it to us.

MASTER QIU: Yes. Please wait a minute. (*Exit.*)

THE PRINCE: (*to* AN QILO) See, cousin, how foolish these people are! In this I'll be impartial. Be you judge of your own case.

(*Enter* MASTER QIU, *followed by* FU QIAOYIN, *veiled.*)

THE PRINCE: Is this the witness, Priest? Let her show her face and then speak.

FU QIAOYIN: Pardon, my lord, I will not show my face until my husband bid me.

THE PRINCE: What? Are you married?

FU QIAOYIN: No.

THE PRINCE: You are a maid then?

FU QIAOYIN: No.

THE PRINCE: A widow, then?

FU QIAOYIN: Neither, my lord.

THE PRINCE: Why, you are nothing then.

LU QIU: My lord, she may be a punk!

THE PRINCE: Silence! The time will soon come for you to speak.

LU QIU: Yes, my lord. (*sticking out his tongue as in fear*)

FU QIAOYIN: My lord, thus it is: I have known my husband, but he

knows not that he knew me.

(*Everybody laughs.*)

THE PRINCE: Why is that?

LU QIU: He was drunk!

THE PRINCE: (*to* LU QIU) One more word and you shall get

twenty lashes!

(LU QIU *shrinks back and covers his mouth with both*

hands.)

(*to* FU QIAOYIN) All right now. To the point: Are you not

to witness for Lord An?

FU QIAOYIN: Yes, my lord. She that accuses him of fornication in

the same way does accuse my husband. But I swear that, at

the time of her accusation, my husband and I were enjoying

full effects of love.

AN QILO: Why, does she charge anyone besides me?

FU QIAOYIN: Not that I know.

THE PRINCE: No? How about your husband?

FU QIAOYIN: Your majesty, that is Lord An.

AN QILO: Am I to endure this? Who are you? Take off your veil!

FU QIAOYIN: Yes, now that my husband commands.

(*She takes off the veil.*)

Do you recognize me now?

THE PRINCE: (*to* AN QILO) Do you know her?

AN QILO: Yes, I do. Frankly, my lord, I was engaged with her, but the contract was long broke off. In the past three years, I haven't spoken one single word to her. These people, my lord, must have been set on. There might be greater conspiracies behind it. Let me have way to find this practice out.

THE PRINCE: Very well. Cousin, do as you think fit.

(THE PRINCE *leaves his seat; to* QUAN SHIKE) My lord Quan, please take this seat.

(QUAN SHIKE *sits down.* THE PRINCE *to* AN QILO *and* QUAN SHIKE) We request your kind pains, both of you, to find out this abuse and punish the false accusers home. Another important business awaits me, but we will be back soon.

AN QILO and **QUAN SHIKE:** (*stand up to see* THE PRINCE *off*) Yes, my lord. We'll do it thoroughly.

(*Exit* THE PRINCE.)

AN QILO: (*to* FU QIAOYIN) Say, who set you on to slander me? Is it that same Daoist priest Master Wen?

FU QIAOYIN: Master Wen did give me instructions, but I've only

told the truth. My lord, my husband, my fickle lover—

(*sings*)

> By ourselves in quiet painted hall,
>
> In moonlight did we our vows exchange.
>
> "Till mountains crumble, oceans dry"—how sweet!
>
> For witness were a pair of lustrous pearls.
>
> Alas, true love is unpredictable.
>
> What did I do to merit your desertion?
>
> My heart's like lotus seed—bitter to the core.
>
> I laugh in public but at home I cry.
>
> No way to keep your love I feel depressed,
>
> Though nightly in my room burns candle red.
>
> I often ask the parrots in the cage:
>
> "Won't you tell me how to spell, O how to spell
>
> 'lovesickness'?"

(*She weeps and wipes tears.*)

AN QILO: You brazen hussy!—

(*sings*)

> Your endless chatter only heaps disgrace
>
> Upon yourself! Your charge is all made up.

My patience here is injurèd by her
Offense against all public decency.

QUAN SHIKE: Bring in Murong Qing.

(*to* AN QILO) My lord, please set your heart at ease and let
me question her. By confronting them we can certainly find
out the truth.

(*Enter two* ATTENDANTS *with* MURONG QING *and two*
other ATTENDANTS *with* THE PRINCE *disguised as*
PRIEST WEN.)

QUAN SHIKE: Hey, are you Priest Wen?

THE PRINCE: That's right.

LU QIU: This is he, for sure!

QUAN SHIKE: Why did you set these two mad women on to
slander Lord An Qilo? They've confessed you did.

THE PRINCE: Rubbish!

QUAN SHIKE: How impudent! Know you this is the court?

THE PRINCE: What court? Where's the Prince? Let me talk to the
Prince.

QUAN SHIKE: The Prince is in us now, Lord An and me. Look you
speak honestly, or we'll charge you with contempt of court.

THE PRINCE: Ah, is the Prince gone?

(*to* MURONG QING *and* FU QIAOYIN) Then is your

cause gone. The Prince is unjust, thus to put your trial in the villain's hand, whom here you come to accuse.

LU QIU: (*steps forward and interrupts*) This is the rascal, my lord. See how impudent he is!

QUAN SHIKE: Hateful wretch! Is it not enough you have suborned these women to accuse an imperially appointed official, but in foul mouth to insult the Prince? Off with him and give him forty lashes!

THE PRINCE: Humph! Hold it. The Prince himself dare not stretch this finger of mine. I'm not his subject. Wandering to this place, I have witnessed licentiousness and lawlessness— signs of decline indeed.

QUAN SHIKE: Huh! Slander of the state! Away with him to prison!

AN QILO: Not so fast. Can you avouch against him, Master Lu?

LU QIU: Sure, my lord.—Come here, Priest Arrogance. Do you know me?

THE PRINCE: So it's you. We met each other at the prison.

LU QIU: Right. And do you remember how you criticized the Prince?

THE PRINCE: Criticize the Prince?

LU QIU: Yeah. With glibness you insulted the Prince by calling him a brothel frequenter, a coward, a fool . . .

THE PRINCE: Eh, I didn't say those things. You indeed spoke so of him, and much more, more worse.

LU QIU: O you baldpate! This is an open lie. Did not I then in anger

pluck you by your ear?

THE PRINCE: I protest I love the Prince as I love myself.

AN QILO: Treasonous blackguard, how dare you quibble!

QUAN SHIKE: Such a fellow is not to be talked with. Away with

him to the prison! Along with those two mad women, too,

and the other confederate companion.

(ATTENDANTS *lay hands on* MURONG QING, FU

QIAOYIN, *and* MASTER QIU.)

THE PRINCE: What's the hurry? Stay a while!

LU QIU: Ha! Do you resist?

(LU QIU *steps forward to assist the* ATTENDANTS.)

(*In chaos,* LU QIU *pulls off* THE PRINCE's *Daoist cap.*)

AN QILO and **QUAN SHIKE:** (*seeing it is* THE PRINCE, *both rise*

and shout) Your Majesty!

(*Everyone looks at each other, not knowing what to do.*)

AN QILO and **QUAN SHIKE:** (*kneel down with the crowd*) Pardon,

my lord!

THE PRINCE: Rise.

(*Everybody rises.*)

(*to* LU QIU) Humph! The audacity to offend the most

powerful!

(*to the attendants*) Lay hold of him.

(*to Lu* QIU) For *that* priest must have a word with you.

LU QIU: O miserable! (*patting his head*) My head . . .

(*Two* ATTENDANTS *step forward to seize* LU QIU *and take him to one side.* MASTER QIU *brings up the crown and* THE PRINCE *puts on his royal robe.*)

THE PRINCE: (*takes the seat, points to* MURONG QING, FU QIAOYIN, *and* MASTER QIU) First, free them.

(*to* QUAN SHIKE) Lord Quan, we pardon you. Sit you down.

As for Lord An, (*to* AN QILO) What word or impudence can serve you now?

AN QILO: Alas—

(*sings an aside*)

His Majesty has caught me unawares.

No more can I defend myself in shame:

One slip and I am trapped in snares I made.

I'll face my death, manlike, with just a sigh.

(*speaks*) My lord, this guilty one is speechless. I should be guiltier than my guiltiness if I persist in deceiving. No longer hold session but let me confess all and then off with my head.

THE PRINCE: All right. Come here, Fu Qiaoyin.—Were you ever
contracted with her?

AN QILO: Yes.

THE PRINCE: Take them hence, let them marry instantly. Lord
Quan, go preside over the marriage and return them here
again.

QUAN SHIKE: Yes, Your Majesty.

(*Exit* QUAN SHIKE, FU QIAOYIN, *followed by* AN QILO
under guard.)

THE PRINCE: (*to* MURONG QING) Lady Murong, though the
priest has turned into a prince, he has not changed heart
with dress. I still have your interest in mind.

MURONG QING: O give me pardon, Your Majesty, that I have put
so much trouble to your unknown sovereignty!

THE PRINCE: You are pardoned, but you must be as generous in
pardoning us. I did not think your brother would be
executed so soon, and it caught me off my guard.

MURONG QING: Alas, it was his poor fate, and not Your Majesty's
fault.

THE PRINCE: It is best to think that way.

(*Enter* QUAN SHIKE, FU QIAOYIN, *and* AN QILO *under*

guard. QUAN SHIKE *returns to his seat.*)

THE PRINCE: An Qilo, first you knowingly broke the law, then you breached a promise. You violated a maiden's chastity and destroyed her reputation. You deceived a higher authority and oppressed the lower people. Such crimes can never be exonerated. "As you sow, so you reap." Like does requite like, and measure still for measure! We do condemn you to death, and with the same haste as Murong Bai's beheading.

FU QIAOYIN: (*shocked, kneels down immediately*) O most gracious lord, do not mock me with a husband!

THE PRINCE: Since I promised to safeguard your honor and right, I have married you to him according to law. To all his possessions, which should be confiscated, we now do you a special favor by making you the heir. If you wish, we could find you a better husband.

FU QIAOYIN: Oh no, my good lord, I do not wish to re-marry.

THE PRINCE: No more of this. We are resolved.

FU QIAOYIN: Merciful lord . . .

THE PRINCE: You are losing your labor! Take him away.

FU QIAOYIN: Please! O my good lord! . . .

(*to* MURONG QING) O, kind sister, won't you help me? Please, put in a word for me. Give him a chance to start anew, please, I beg of you . . .

THE PRINCE: (*sternly*) He dies for Murong Bai's death.

FU QIAOYIN: Sweet Sister Murong, say nothing, but do kneel by

> me . . .

THE PRINCE: Should she kneel down, it would be most unfair to

> her wronged brother. How could *he* rest in peace in the
>
> underworld?

MURONG QING: (*gazes first at* FU QIAOYIN, *then at* AN QILO;

> *slowly kneels down; determinedly*) Your Majesty, please
>
> spare this man. After all—my brother was at fault; he had
>
> but justice according to the law. For An Qilo—his act did
>
> not overtake his bad intent. Thus let it be considered as
>
> mere intent. A due sincerity, I think, governed his deeds,
>
> till he did look on me. . . . My lord, I beg you to be
>
> magnanimous—
>
> (*sings*)

> No sages, we are prone to make mistakes;
> There is no greater good than to reform.
> Unhappy is the fate of my brother, true,
> But yet he did the thing for which he died.
> Kind sovereigns take precautions from the start;
> To punish without warning is tyranny.

Confer extensive benefits to all;

Solicit good advice and welcome wisdom.

Imbue the world with worthy teaching, and

Halcyon days are bound to follow.

THE PRINCE: (*deeply moved; aside*) The trick that saved Murong
Bai I hid from her on purpose, to test her. And now these
words—

(*sings an aside*)

She spoke with eloquence, authority.

Her words are plain, her meaning most profound.

With clemency she answers good for evil.

Intelligence she has, as well as looks.

Awakened suddenly to recent fault,

Henceforth virtuous men alone will I install.

This time I'll pardon him at her request,

And seek a happy marriage preordained.

(*speaks*) Stand up, both of you. We will make a final
decision later. Now, where is Lord Dian?

(FU QIAOYIN *and* FU QIAOYIN *stand up.*)

LORD DIAN: (*steps forward*) Yes, Your Majesty.

THE PRINCE: Why did Murong Bai's execution take place at an
unusual hour? Do you not know it was unlawful?

LORD DIAN: Yes, Your Majesty, I do admit it.

THE PRINCE: (*knowingly*) For this we do move you down three grades and withhold your salary for one year.

LORD DIAN: I humbly thank Your Majesty. Yet I did take an expedient measure concerning this case, and kept the testimonies.

THE PRINCE: Oh? Show them.

LORD DIAN: Yes, Your Majesty.

    (*He gestures, and an* OFFICER *enters with* MURONG BAI, *muffled.*)

LORD DIAN: Here, my lord, is the evidence.

    (*He unmuffles* MURONG BAI, *to the astonishment of the crowd, who starts to whisper to one another.*)

MURONG QING: (*shouts in surprise*) My dear brother!

MURONG BAI: My sister!

    (*They hug each other, weeping.*)

THE PRINCE: We hereby pardon Murong Bai, and An Qilo.

    (*to* MURONG BAI) Choose a propitious day for your marriage as soon as possible.

    (*to* AN QILO) And you—see that you reform yourself anew.

    (*points to* MURONG BAI *and* AN QILO) Now that you've

escaped death, be sure to remember the lesson and offend no more. From now on husband and wife should be of one heart and always show due respect to each other.

MURONG BAI and **AN QILO:** I humbly thank Your Majesty.

THE PRINCE: (*glances at* LU QIU) Only one person here I cannot forgive.

(*to* LU QIU) It's your turn now. Sirrah, know you the offense of slandering your prince?

LU QIU: O my gracious lord, I spoke it but according to the reports in *The Mango Tabloid.* Please, my magnanimous lord, do not take it seriously.

THE PRINCE: Your slander we can forgive, but see that you formally marry Spring Charm, the girl whom you made pregnant.

LU QIU: O Your Majesty, please, be so kind as not to make a whore my wife! That is whipping plus lingering death—even worse than beheading.

THE PRINCE: Slandering a prince deserves it. Off with him! You must marry her.

(*Exit* LU QIU *under guard.*)

LU QIU: (*shouts as he exits*) Would no one put in a good word for me? Lord Shakespeare! . . .

THE PRINCE: Lord Quan and Lord Dian, you two have taken good

care of business. We shall reward you accordingly.

QUAN SHIKE and **LORD DIAN:** I humbly thank Your Majesty.

THE PRINCE: Lady Murong, I have yet another word for you—

(*walks toward* MURONG QING)

(*sings*)

> **A red plum placed in crystal ice, you are**
>
> **Translucent, your virtue spreading wide.**
>
> **Endowed with natural beauty and intelligence,**
>
> **You've also drunk deep from scholarship.**
>
> **Most rare's the magnanimity you've shown:**
>
> **You win with gentleness—a model clear.**
>
> **Would you be my queen and reign with me,**
>
> **A dragon and a phoenix—a perfect pair?**

MURONG QING: (*stunned*) Ah? Well . . .

THE PRINCE: (*gently*) There's no rush. We can talk about it later.

(*to the* ATTENDANTS) Come, we will return to the court.

(*Exeunt all according to their ranks, except* MURONG

QING, *who stays onstage, as if lost in thought.*)

(*Light dims.*)

Epilogue

Location: A thoroughfare in the Kingdom of Nanping.

(*Enter some* ATTENDANTS *to post a proclamation. As a crowd gathers to see what's going on,* THE PRINCE *arrives with* QUAN SHIKE *and other* OFFICIALS*; they chat leisurely with people—a perfect picture of peace and prosperity.*)

[Chorus]

Harsh laws abolished, order all brought back,

With prudence I apply both grace and mulct;

With care I find out truth from lies of men;

For public posts I pick the virtuous

And able. Judging on one's own's so shallow!

With tact we remove evil, hail the good.

With charity we care for common men;

A liberal mind does make a spacious world.

The End

量・度

（改編自莎士比亞 *Measure for Measure*）

彭鏡禧　著
陳　芳

臺灣 學ㄓ書局 印行

國家圖書館出版品預行編目資料

MEASURE, MEASURE! 量‧度

彭鏡禧、陳芳著. – 初版. – 臺北市：臺灣學生，2012.06
面；公分

ISBN 978-957-15-1564-9 (平裝)

854.5   101009809

MEASURE, MEASURE! 量‧度

著　作　者：彭　鏡　禧　　、　　陳　　芳
出　版　者：臺　灣　學　生　書　局　有　限　公　司
發　行　人：楊　　　　雲　　　　龍
發　行　所：臺　灣　學　生　書　局　有　限　公　司
　　　　　　臺北市和平東路一段七十五巷十一號
　　　　　　郵 政 劃 撥 帳 號：0 0 0 2 4 6 6 8
　　　　　　電　話：（0 2）2 3 9 2 8 1 8 5
　　　　　　傳　眞：（0 2）2 3 9 2 8 1 0 5
　　　　　　E-mail：student.book@msa.hinet.net
　　　　　　http：//www.studentbook.com.tw
本 書 局 登
記 證 字 號：行政院新聞局局版北市業字第玖捌壹號
印　刷　所：長　欣　印　刷　企　業　社
　　　　　　新北市中和區永和路三六三巷四二號
　　　　　　電　話：（0 2）2 2 2 6 8 8 5 3

定價：新臺幣二五○元

西　元　二　○　一　二　年　六　月　初　版

ISBN 978-957-15-1564-9

《量・度》由臺灣豫劇團首演
（與春之聲管弦樂團聯演）
時間：2012 年 6 月 8 日 19：30
地點：臺灣臺北市國家戲劇院

導演	呂柏伸
副導演	殷青群
指揮	陳永清
音樂設計	耿玉卿
配器	李宏權
服裝設計	李育昇
舞臺設計	張哲龍
燈光設計	JACK
南平王／文道長	王海玲
慕容青	蕭揚玲
安其樂	劉建華
權世可	朱海珊
典大人	殷青群
符巧茵	謝文琪
慕容白	張翊生
丘道長	林文瑋
盧迷	鄭曉巍
老鴇	蕭揚珍
向隅	胡昌民

何保生	楊原青
妓女若干人	傅瑞雲、張揚蘭、孫儀婷、陳美玲
嫖客若干人	張揚忠、林原茂、楊原青

情與理，男與女，罪與罰
怎樣量度《量·度》

王德威
中央研究院院士
哈佛大學講座教授

　　《量·度》是彭鏡禧教授與陳芳教授合作改編自莎士比亞戲劇 *Measure for Measure* 的「豫莎劇」，由臺灣豫劇團製作公演。彭教授與陳教授曾經合作將莎翁的《威尼斯商人》（*The Merchant of Venice*）改為劇本《約／束》，由臺灣豫劇皇后、國家文藝獎得主王海玲女士率團主演，極獲好評。《量·度》再接再厲，自然令觀眾期盼。

　　莎士比亞在 1604 年完成劇作 *Measure for Measure*。這齣戲有陰錯陽差的巧合、皆大歡喜的結局，歷來被歸類為喜劇。但是戲中有關倫理、法律、欲望的情節錯綜複雜，已經超過表面嬉笑怒罵的向度，因此也常常被視為莎翁的「問題劇」。現代中國莎劇翻譯家朱生豪將這齣戲譯為《一報還一報》，梁實秋則譯為《惡有惡報》，都意在點出戲中善惡消長和中國傳統「果報」關係的對應。但是「報」的觀念未必完全說明莎翁創作的複雜面

向。彭鏡禧教授翻譯此劇，並命名為《量·度》，顯然希望以比較中性的詞彙點出原作對人性關係的微妙省思。

《量·度》中南平王暫離王位，由攝政安其樂掌權。安其樂執法嚴峻，查禁城中風月場所，引來「哀鴻遍野」。他更要處死慕容白，罪名是讓未婚妻懷孕。慕容白的姐姐慕容青已有意在道觀皈依，為了營救弟弟，請見安其樂求情，未料觸動後者欲望，反而要求慕容青自動獻身，以貞操作為交換條件。這讓慕容青陷入艱難的考驗：她應該屈從安其樂的欲望，營救弟弟的性命？或者信守清規戒律，一任至親之人受死？一場好戲，由此開始。

乍看之下，《量·度》雜糅了小兒女的浪漫情事、為政者的法理威權、出家人的清貞決絕、還有市井男女的插科打諢，形成有驚無險的喜劇。然而細心的觀眾不難發覺，這齣戲一波又一波的高潮其實建立在一場又一場的危機上，而危機之後的轉機與其說解決了問題，不如說帶來一種恐怖平衡。置身其間，各個人物所做出的回應靠的不只是判斷力，也是運氣。這使全劇情節充滿曖昧性。而如何計算得與失，就有賴觀眾的度量了。

安其樂與慕容青的對立是全劇首要張力所在。安其樂自詡剛正不阿，執法如山，他將掃黃措施擴大為愛情糾察，甚至已有婚約的男女也在監管範圍。安其樂雖然師出有名，但他的作為已經有了剛愎苛虐之嫌。他要處死慕容白，以理殺人，莫此為甚。寫作《老殘遊記》的劉鶚嘗嘆「清官比贓官更可怕」，因為清官自以為無所求，因此可以無所不為，此之謂也。

所幸《量·度》是喜劇，越是道貌岸然的大人先生，越要讓他露出馬腳。安其樂一見美人立刻打回原形，轉變之快，寧非怪

事。但他對慕容青所提出的交換條件卻又導致另一場危機。他所暴露的不只是飲食男女的人之大慾，同時也是自己的偽善矯情。當慕容青拒絕了安其樂的要求，與其說她要保持對神佛守貞的信念，更不如說她要保持對人性誠信的最後底線。法理不外人情，宗教也不外人情。

就在眾人一籌莫展之際，喬裝改扮的南平王適時現身搭救。他的方法不外是將錯就錯，移花接木。以此這般，慕容青倖免受辱，安其樂作繭自縛，慕容白也在千鈞一髮之際刀下留人。《量·度》最後不負眾望，以喜劇收場。但觀眾不禁要問，如果沒有南平王的介入，劇情又將如何？

安其樂在劇中儘管是眾矢之的，但以仁君出現的南平王恐怕才真正難辭其咎。南平王治下法鬆紀弛，不正是滿城春色的始作俑者？何況他的重用安其樂，顯然沒有識人之明。不論是莎翁原稿或者是改編以後的《量·度》都強調天理、人欲之間必須求乎中道，否則勢必產生像安其樂這樣過猶不及的例子。然而知易畢竟行難，南平王果真能擺平一切？

這就讓我們進一步觀察這齣戲最要著墨的愛情故事。慕容白與未婚妻因為婚前懷孕而致罪，雖然顯得無辜，但從道學眼光來看，他們的確破壞了「規矩」，因此怨不得人。只是量刑的輕重，影響了全劇道德砝碼的平衡。莎翁對人間情事顯然沒有太大信心。南平王的國度裏風花雪月，說明了欲望的純任天然，也說明了欲望的沒有歸宿。安其樂未必是人面獸心之徒，只是刻意「克己復禮」，遇到誘惑反而醜態畢露。在南平王巧計之下，他沒能玷辱慕容青，卻與原來已被他拋棄的未婚妻成其好事。這算

一報還一報了。劇情終了，還有兩段轉折，好色客盧述被判明媒正娶被他睡大了肚子的妓女；而南平王自己對慕容青似乎產生情愫。

　　莎士比亞對人性的幽微面洞若觀火，在《量·度》這樣的喜劇裏選擇高高舉起，輕輕打下，務求皆大歡喜。但欲望的問題其實沒有解決，何況理法？如果從性別角度來看，我們更要說，「量度」的標準其實是以男性欲望滿足與否為出發點。慕容青的危機因為安其樂而起，到了最後並不因為南平王而止，為這齣戲留下不能讓人安心的伏筆。安其樂沒有得到所欲的獵物，反而被迫娶了他休掉的未婚妻。但這算是他的懲罰麼？在簡單的情愛的邏輯裏也許是。果然如此，這位未婚妻又如何安頓自己的位置？她到底算是勝利奪回婚約，還是被用為懲罰安其樂的工具？或是開脫他失去慕容青的「安慰獎」？我們不曾忘記，當初安其樂休未婚妻的原因是女方家長海難，盡數失去家產。

　　我們於是來到罪與罰的問題。論者早已指出這齣戲在法的認知和實踐方面的曖昧不明之處。人治和法制、神恩和君權，糾纏不清。在此之上，是莎士比亞所關心的欲望和律法之間的辯證關係。既然人之大欲沛然莫之能禦，我們就必須虛心回應。設立律法，不過是其中之一端，更重要的是如前所述，在情與理之間審時度勢，量刑以對。

　　但弔詭的是，沒有對法的逾越，不足以顯示法的存在和權威。安其樂的整頓風月，以致打算處死慕容白，均可如是觀。但另一方面，他自己知法犯法，是否就更應該罪加一等？全劇的發展顯然不是如此。更微妙的是，南平王自己何嘗不是在非常時

機，運用非常手段，來解決安其樂的濫用法令所帶來的危機？既然貴為一國之君，國法的仲裁者，南平王似乎師出有名。但他的「便宜行事」一方面坐實君權的無上權威，另一方面也顛覆了法的自足性——間接也就解構君王自己的權威。《量·度》劇中，表面是對情、理、法面面俱到，實則是以未必圓滿的婚禮、心照不宣的妥協，來解決已經存在的情與法，罪與罰二律悖反的問題。

　　閱讀《量·度》因此再一次讓我們體會莎士比亞原作的複雜程度與包容性，以及兩位翻譯、改編者的用心。從十七世紀的英國伊麗莎白時代劇場到二十一世紀臺灣的豫劇演出，時空、語言、文化背景的穿越與逾越不在話下。而《量·度》的可觀，正是來自於翻譯者、改編者、製作者與演出團隊的不斷仔細揣摩、演繹、再現不同語境的異同。一方面忠於原典精神，一方面發展在地風格，一方面力求符合劇種特色。長短輕重，必須妥為因應。measure for measure—— 不正是「量度」的一大考驗？

弁　言

　　莎士比亞（William Shakespeare, 1564-1616）戲劇大多是改編（不是原創），透過各種繁複的修辭技巧或文字遊戲，其思想深度與人物塑造，都令人印象深刻。由於種種內、外在因素，莎劇不但屹立於世界劇壇，成為當代眾所周知的經典，更是跨文化劇場的最愛。如果要把莎劇改編到中國戲曲的表演樣式中，會如何轉化呢？

　　中國戲曲是歷史悠久的程式性劇場；唱念化的語言、虛擬化的身段、類型化的行當、象徵化的臉譜、寫意化的舞美，在當代劇場各種創新思維中，又要如何體現莎劇的語言魅力、劇情張力，乃至人物複雜深沈的心性？「豫莎劇」《量・度》（改編自 *Measure for Measure*）會呈現什麼樣的跨文化風景？在在考驗著主創團隊的「量度」。

　　但就文本而言，原著劇名典出聖經《新約・馬太福音》七章 2 節，似乎是警惕世人：切莫論斷他人，以免自己也被同樣的標準論斷。全劇表面上高舉著法理的大纛，其實卻充滿了對於「食、色，性也」的理解和同情。歷來中譯劇名如《一報還一報》、《惡有惡報》、《請君入甕》、《知法犯法》、《作法自斃》、《自作自受》、《將心比心》、《量罪記》等，可能都無

法全面觀照箇中的深層意涵。本劇正名為《量·度》，也是希望呼應其慎重斷案、合乎中道（動詞 measure = consider, calculate；名詞 measure = moderation, temperance）的量罪與寬恕主旨。而在文化移轉及語言對焦上，則多所思考「存神遺形」的跨界空間。

衷心感謝導演呂柏伸兄提供寶貴意見，王德威教授於百忙中為本書作序，瀞暄精心設計封面，臺灣豫劇團慷慨提供劇照、曲譜。期待《量·度》能與讀者／觀眾產生對話。

目　錄

《量・度》

改編自莎士比亞 *Measure for Measure*
彭鏡禧、陳芳

人物表

南平王	南平國國王
慕容青	慕容白之姐，一位親信弟子
安其樂	攝政，代理南平王
權世可	丞相
典大人	大理寺卿，兼掌牢獄
符巧茵	符將軍之妹，原是安其樂之未婚妻
慕容白	家道中落之書香子弟
丘道長	沖虛觀道長
文道長	遊方道長（南平王喬裝）
盧述	花花公子
老鴇	怡春院老闆
向隅	窰子龜奴，兼差酒保
何保生	牢獄中之劊子手
妓女若干人	
嫖客若干人	
百姓若干人	

公差若干人
官員若干人

場 目

序　曲

（地點：南平王國市衢大道）
（眾百姓圍觀新貼告示，指指點點，議論紛紛）

【伴唱】：王爺悄悄離都城，
　　　　　攝政代理法嚴明。
　　　　　苦口良藥下得猛，
　　　　　半信半疑人人驚；
　　　　　半信半疑人人驚。

第一場　違法

（接〈序曲〉）

盧述：　哇！本城所有的窰子都要拆除了，片瓦不留啊。

嫖客甲：喂！你們看清楚了，這上頭說，連「一樓一鳳」也不准哪……

嫖客乙：這樣太嚴厲了吧？你們說，這一回到底是玩真的還是假的？

嫖客甲：誰知道呢！王爺有沒有看到這個告示？

盧述：　當然沒有！王爺出城去進行「秘密外交」了——

眾人：　什麼秘密？什麼外交？

嫖客甲：你怎麼知道？

盧述：　哼！有什麼是我盧述不知道的事兒！
　　　　　王爺啊，這會兒正忙著哪。他聯合了東華王、西岐王一起去找北唐主談判；假如談不攏，就要出兵攻打北唐了。

老鴇：　哎唷，像這樣，又是戰爭，又是瘟疫，又是拆房子，老娘的生意都淡出鳥啦。

妓女甲：就是說嘛。郭大戶已有半個月沒上門了，蔡官人也不見人影了……他們以前可都是天天來玩兒的呀！

妓女乙：如今呢，可是連王二麻子都懶得到咱們這條鶯花巷來叫賣——威而剛了。

老鴇：　看來年頭真的不一樣了！再這麼著，我可怎麼好哪？

盧述：　　得啦！你擔什麼心！「怡春院」改個招貼，繼續幹老本
　　　　　行啊。比方說——改成「回春堂」，換湯不換藥嘛！
　　　　　（龜奴向隅衝上）

向隅：　　媽媽！（上氣不接下氣）那邊，那邊，（手指上場門）
　　　　　有人被抓啦……

老鴇：　　慌什麼？是哪個啊？

向隅：　　是慕容公子啊！

眾人：　　（驚愕狀，七嘴八舌）什麼？慕容公子？

老鴇：　　他一個倒抵得上你們五千個！（向向隅）你這消息可靠
　　　　　麼？

向隅：　　當然可靠！我正在介壽門外大街拉皮條，親眼看著典大
　　　　　人帶人去抓他呢。而且，上頭傳下話來，三日內就要問
　　　　　斬啦。

眾人：　　（驚愕狀，七嘴八舌）什麼？問斬？

盧述：　　難怪他約了我一個時辰前在這兒見面，卻到現在還沒
　　　　　來。他可是個志誠君子，從來不失信的啊。

老鴇：　　（向向隅）幹嘛抓他呀？

向隅：　　為了一位姑娘。

盧述：　　他犯了什麼罪？

向隅：　　不該在私有的小溪裡摸鱸魚。那個姑娘呀……（比畫一
　　　　　個大肚子）

盧述：　　哦，有喜啦？儘管這麼胡搞瞎搞，也不致於淪落到問斬
　　　　　的下場吧？

眾人：　　（點頭附和）是啊，是啊。

老鴇： 是啊，這打什麼要緊！媽媽我這兒的姑娘，要是不小心懷了孩子，大不了就送到──怡春院附設托兒所……這也是咱們東家企業化經營的一種福利嘛……

（上場門傳來嘈雜聲，眾人望去）

向隅： 嘿，瞧，那不就是慕容公子嗎？

（大理寺卿典大人率二公差押解慕容白上）

慕容白：典大人，何須如此費事？讓小民帶著枷鎖遊街示眾！直接把我關入大牢裡，也就是了。

典大人：慕容公子，不是本官有意作難於你，這可是攝政爺的特別旨令啊。

慕容白：人哪，一朝大權在握，就如同神明了，能夠操控罪人的生死。高興怎麼著，就怎麼著。無論判決輕重，他總是有理的。唉！

盧述： （一個箭步衝上，對典大人不住地打躬作揖）典大人，行個方便，容小民說兩句話。

（典大人揮手同意，退立一旁）

盧述： （對慕容白）賢弟，怎麼回事？你怎麼會落到這種光景？

慕容白：啊，盧兄。這是因為太過於恣意任性，太過於隨心所欲了。一不留神，就踰越了規矩，觸犯了禁忌。就像老鼠貪吃，誤食毒餌，終歸斃命。人性亦然；為了渴求滿足，也顧不得那許多了。

盧述： （旁白）哈！他倒了大楣，竟還能有這番說辭……書呆子！（向慕容白）你到底犯了什麼罪啊？

慕容白：盧兄啊──您知道小弟早已與表妹指腹為婚。只因家

　　　　貧，故而尚未迎娶，就先入了洞房。不料，一晌貪歡，
　　　　卻暗結珠胎……

盧述：　那就趕緊把喜事辦一辦，親上加親，雙喜臨門，也就罷
　　　　了。

慕容白：小弟原是這麼打算的。不過，尚未納徵，這位攝政爺就
　　　　忽然祭出嚴刑峻法，我也就這麼被冠上了淫蕩私通的罪
　　　　名。

盧述：　唔，新官上任三把火啊！

慕容白：那可不？攝政爺他——

　　　　（唱）初掌大權著新袍，

　　　　　　　雷厲風行野火燒。

　　　　　　　詔書輕易下一道，

　　　　　　　人如草芥性命拋。

　　　　　　　官樣文章將我套，

　　　　　　　分明是——沽名釣譽在今朝。

盧述：　你的腦袋看來是搖搖晃晃了。快去找王爺求情啊。

慕容白：（垂頭喪氣）小弟也是這麼想，可就沒處找去——誰知
　　　　道王爺的下落呢？

盧述：　這倒是。

　　　　（旁白）我只知道王爺出城去了，再要我瞎編下去，我
　　　　也沒詞兒了。

典大人：（催促著）好了，該走了。誤了時辰，攝政爺可不會輕
　　　　饒哪。

慕容白：再說一句，大人，一句就好。

　　　　（向盧述）盧兄，好歹請您幫個大忙。

盧述：　你說。

慕容白：家姐日前剛去修真觀，思量著在那兒潛心修道呢。她可
　　　　不是一般的女子啊，她啊——

　　　　（唱）青春年華多窈窕，

　　　　　　　花容月貌分外嬌。

　　　　　　　能言善道心思巧，

　　　　　　　知書達禮識見高。

　　　　　　　逢凶化吉恩典討，

　　　　　　　全仗青姐走一遭。

　　　　（白）盧兄，可否勞駕您跑一趟修真觀，帶個口信給她？
　　　　請她速去向攝政爺求個情吧。

盧述：　沒問題，包在愚兄身上。這不僅是為了你，也是為普天
　　　　之下的男人請命啊。要不然，只因木杵搗了石臼，就得
　　　　賠上性命，這也未免 too much 了。我這就去。

慕容白：多謝盧兄。

　　　　（向典大人）走吧，大人。

　　　　（典大人率二公差押解慕容白下）

　　　　（切光）

第二場　喬裝

（地點：沖虛觀內）

（南平王、丘道長正在密談）

南平王： 丘道長，本王對外宣稱已前往北唐處理公務，並安排安
其樂大人暫代攝政，其實是另有深意的。

丘道長： 小道願聞其詳，王爺請說。

南平王： 道長啊，自古來——

　　　　（唱）明君有術威名顯，

　　　　　　　治大國如烹小鮮。

　　　　　　　脫韁野馬跑不遠，

　　　　　　　馴服只要霸王鞭。

　　　　　　　可嘆我、宅心仁厚存善念，

　　　　　　　嚴峻典律任高懸。

　　　　　　　而今積重甚難返，

　　　　　　　道德斲喪一瞬間。

　　　　　　　改弦更張當機斷，

　　　　　　　借風且推順水船。

　　　　（白）所以，本王要借重安大人的長才，好好整飭一番。

丘道長： 但是，王爺隨時可以恢復律法的效力啊，何須假手他人？

南平王：（擺擺手）不然。本國的百姓啊——

　　　　（唱）敝善飾非無忌憚，

　　　　姑息在我理不端。

　　　　雷霆陡降招民怨，

　　　　何如袖手壁上觀。

　　（白）安大人哪，就是本王的一枚活棋。本王多年來放縱百姓，從未稍加管束。現今民風淫亂，人心不古，本王實難卸責。此時若重申律令，恐怕百姓不服，徒增困擾。（停頓）安大人一向嚴以律己，鐵面無私。代理攝政，應可賞罰分明，警世醒眾，為我分憂。

丘道長：王爺真是用心良苦。

南平王：本王還有一事相煩。

丘道長：王爺但請吩咐，小道定當遵命。

南平王：本王有意立即改扮裝束，和你以道兄相稱，請你掩護。這是為了便於察訪民隱，一併觀察安大人的舉措，能否改良社會風氣。

丘道長：是，小道這就去準備。請您稍候。（下）

南平王：（沉思片刻）安其樂啊、安其樂，如今已賜你權柄，願你能助本王一臂之力。本王拭目以待。

　　（切光）

第三場　祈請

（地點：公堂議事廳）

（安其樂、權世可正在討論公務。一公差引典大人上）

公差：　　啟稟大人，大理寺卿典有道求見。

安其樂：傳。

（典大人入內，施禮）

安其樂：有事麼？典大人。

典大人：大人，下官……下官特地前來請示：明日午時三刻，當
　　　　真要處決慕容白麼？

安其樂：哼！你沒收到旨令麼？何須多問！

典大人：大人恕罪，下官不敢違令。只是……此事太過於倉促，
　　　　本朝從無這等先例。下官以為……大人或許會改變心
　　　　意，故此……

權世可：是啊！安大人，這慕容白還是已故慕容縣令的獨生子
　　　　啊。慕容縣令當年素有官聲，頗得百姓愛戴。何況——
　　　　（唱）為政之道在寬柔，
　　　　　　　甘棠仁愛古遺風。
　　　　　　　人命關天宜慎重，
　　　　　　　何妨三思而後行？

安其樂：（轉向權世可）權大人，我們絕不能把律法當作稻草人！
　　　　（唱）身負重任乾坤整，

　　　　不懼誹謗不計名。

　　　　立威豈能圖僥倖？

　　　　懲一儆百建奇功。

　（冷峻）典大人，律法可不是虛文，本官代理攝政，也不是兒戲。

　（續唱）知法犯法理不容，

　　　　　絕不枉法徇私情。

　　　　　罰薄難治膏肓病，

　　　　　誅嚴方能玉宇清。

權世可：大人您——

　（唱）潔身自愛如明鏡，

　　　　白珪無瑕不染塵。

　　　　一旦機緣天作弄，

　　　　尤雲殢雨兩歡濃。

　（白）到那時節呵，

　（接唱）莫非請君自入甕？

　（白）大人哪——

　（接唱）將心比心存善終。

安其樂：權大人何出此言？這慕容白啊——

　（唱）目無法紀有鐵證，

　　　　何須計較口舌爭？

　　　　就事論事該償命，

　　　　無端臆測你有何憑？

　　　　若有一朝我春心動，

　　　　　　（停頓，斬釘截鐵的語氣）

　　　　　　（接唱）依法量刑也相同。

　　　　　　（白）慕容白，定斬不赦！

權世可：大人，……

安其樂：（以手勢阻止權世可）不必多言了。

　　　　　　（一公差上）

公差：　啟稟大人，外頭有一位姑娘，自稱是罪囚慕容白的姐姐，
　　　　求見大人。

安其樂：咦？他有姐姐？

典大人：是，大人。慕容小姐秀外慧中，聽說她在父母雙亡後，
　　　　潛心研習道經；現在是一名親信弟子。

安其樂：哦，喚她進來。

公差：　是。（下）

慕容青：（內唱）度關山、涉險灘，

　　　　　　　　　連夜趲行辭道觀。

　　　　　　（公差在前引路，盧述上；慕容青隨後）

　　　　　　（接唱）多少紅杏枝頭掩，

　　　　　　　　　　夾道翠柳不忍看。

　　　　　　　　　　山雨欲來風雲變，

　　　　　　　　　　救弟惟有一寸丹。

慕容青、盧述：（入內，施禮）見過大人。

安其樂：嗯，有什麼事？

慕容青：大人，民女是來求情的。

安其樂：求什麼情？

慕容青：大人，此一敗德之罪，實實令人難以啟齒。我本不願為
　　　　此前來求情，但又不得不來。

安其樂：哦？為了何事？

慕容青：舍弟慕容白已被判處死刑。

安其樂：嗯，慕容白。

慕容青：是。民女懇請大人，責罰其罪而莫責罰其人。

安其樂：什麼？責罪不責人？哼！豈有此理！果然依你所言，怪
　　　　罪明文規定的刑責，卻縱放人犯，那還要我這個攝政做
　　　　什麼呢？

慕容青：啊！公正但嚴苛的律法！可憐的白弟！（退後一步，待
　　　　轉身）

盧述：　（急向慕容青低語）不能就這樣放棄！去求他啊！你太
　　　　冷漠了。就算是乞討一根針，也要有點兒熱情嘛。去啊！

慕容青：（上前）他非死不可嗎？

安其樂：無法更改。

慕容青：民女知道您可以赦免他。上天有好生之德。順應自然之
　　　　道，也是合乎輿情的啊。

安其樂：本官不願如此。

慕容青：但您可以的，如果您願意，不是嗎？

安其樂：太遲了，已然宣判了。

盧述：　（再向慕容青低語）你的語氣太平淡了。

慕容青：太遲了？哦，不會的。大人，您有權勢可以生殺予奪，
　　　　但慈悲卻是您最珍貴的恩典啊。如果您與舍弟易地而

　　　　　處，您也會犯他的錯，他可就不會這麼嚴峻了。

盧述：　　（又向慕容青低語）對，去感動他，就像這樣。

安其樂：（揮手）令弟必須受到律法的制裁。你這是白費唇舌。

慕容青：但願上天把您的權柄賜給我，而您卻是民女，那麼，情
　　　　　勢會是這樣嗎？不，我會體認到兩者的不同。

安其樂：沒有什麼不同。是律法判處令弟的死罪，不是本官。即
　　　　　使他是本官的兄弟，也不能改變這個判決。明日就要行
　　　　　刑。

慕容青：明日？啊！太突然了！赦免他吧！他還這麼年輕。大人
　　　　　——

　　　（唱）天道好生妙入神，
　　　　　　滋潤萬物總回春。
　　　　　　積德只要懷惻隱，
　　　　　　為善不過一點仁。
　　　　　　舉步尚看蟲蟻徑，
　　　　　　禁火莫燒密山林。
　　　　　　物我兼容有慈愍，
　　　　　　君子任德不任刑。
　　　　　　歸真返璞遵古訓，
　　　　　　教化為先無棄人。

安其樂：你何必說這番大道理？

慕容青：大人，即使是替天行道，也不該如此輕率啊！請您想想，
　　　　　以前可有什麼人是為了這種罪過而死？多的是犯這種罪
　　　　　的！

盧述：　　（向慕容青低語）對，說得好！

安其樂：本官承認，過去律法只是像稻草人擺個樣子而已——但並沒有廢除。

慕容青：請您發發慈悲吧。

安其樂：彰顯法理就是本官的慈悲，那是悲憫尚未犯罪的人。信賞必罰，理所當然。誅惡懲凶，以昭炯戒，才能遏止更多的罪行。

　　　　（唱）補偏救弊主意定，

　　　　　　　六親不認依法行。

　　　　　　　勸善懲惡操權柄，

　　　　　　　移風易俗百廢興。

　　　　（白）明日一定要處決令弟。

慕容青：啊，大人，擁有生殺大權固然威風，但濫用這種權力可就是暴虐了。大人——

　　　　（唱）人生一場黃粱夢，

　　　　　　　鏡花水月原是空。

　　　　　　　聖人無名無所用，

　　　　　　　風行草偃物自榮。

　　　　　　　矯枉亦須持中正，

　　　　　　　切莫過甚傷天功。

安其樂：（似有所感）呀！這……

　　　　（旁唱）春雷驀然響一聲，

　　　　　　　　久蟄寒蚩暗心驚。

　　　　　　　　彷彿今朝夢初醒，

　　　　　　　且自凝神側耳聽。

盧述：　（旁白）看來攝政爺快回心轉意了……

權世可：（旁白）但願她能說服安大人。

慕容青：天生萬物各有不同，我們不能用自己的標準去衡量別人
　　　　哪。

　　　　（唱）萬物各自有本性，

　　　　　　　量度豈能任我行？

　　　　　　　燕雀不知圖南境，

　　　　　　　夏蟲難以語寒冰。

　　　　　　　州官放火神氣定，

　　　　　　　未許百姓點燭燈。

　　　　　　　捫心自問您反躬省，

　　　　　　　可曾動念——情獨鍾？

　　　　（白）大人，如您也曾順乎本性，起過心念，就請赦免
　　　　他的死罪吧。

安其樂：（向眾人）好吧，本官會考量這件案子。各位都請回吧。

　　　　（向慕容青）你明早再來。

慕容青：（微感欣喜）是，多謝大人。願大人洪福齊天。

權世可、典大人：　我等告退。

　　　　（眾人下）

安其樂：（苦笑）洪福齊天？這是怎麼了？我一向克己復禮，奉
　　　　公守法，從未踰矩。然而今日，卻這般把持不住——

　　　　（唱）伊人她端方秀雅聲清朗，

　　　　　　　色絕天下並無雙。

　　　　　伊人她言辭肯綮見識廣，

　　　　　字字珠璣舌如簧。

　　　　　可憐我如癡如醉心盪漾，

　　　　　七情六慾沒主張。

　　　　　可憐我坐立難安癡癡想，

　　　　　心猿意馬好徬徨。

　　　　　此情此景俱難忘，

　　　　　是殺是赦——費思量、費思量。

　　（安其樂微微搖頭，甚感苦惱）

　　（切光）

第四場　私訪

（地點：牢獄）

（典大人手持密件與喬裝成道長的南平王上）

典大人：文道長，如此看來，王爺的意思（指密件）是要安排您
　　　　　來視察牢獄的麼？

南平王：呃，大人言重了。王爺不過是讓小道來此祈福解厄、祓
　　　　　除不祥，順道開示死囚。……呃，請教，最近有無特別
　　　　　案例？

典大人：是有一例，道長。前任慕容縣令的公子——慕容白，因
　　　　　為讓他未過門的媳婦有了喜，被攝政爺判處死刑，不日
　　　　　就要問斬了。

南平王：哦？有這等事？讓我跟慕容公子談談。

典大人：是，請隨我來。

　　　　　（典大人引領南平王行至慕容白的牢房）

　　　　　（叫喚公差）打開牢門！

　　　　　（公差開門）

典大人：慕容公子，這位文道長有話要對你說。

慕容白：（無精打采）有什麼好說的？除非是攝政爺赦免了我的
　　　　　死罪！

　　　　　（南平王作個手勢，典大人領首，下）

南平王：看來你很期待得到赦免令？

慕容白：不幸的人別無選擇，只能期待。唉！

南平王：你要豁達些，做好赴死的準備。那麼，無論生死，都可
以坦然接受了。你要明白——

（唱）　六合本是一芥子，

　　　　糾纏世俗太無知。

　　　　執象以求殫心智，

　　　　汲汲營營歲月移。

　　　　身不由己忘所以，

　　　　百般無奈終歸一。

　　　　死亦生來生亦死，

　　　　物我兩忘與天齊。

（白）所以，了悟大道，超越生死，才是你現在應該思
考的課題。

慕容白：啊！多謝道長開示。但生死這等大事——

（唱）　說來容易實不易，

　　　　姑妄言之姑聽之。

　　　　未知生來焉知死，

　　　　惘然將信復將疑。

南平王：（取出《太平經》交給慕容白，接唱）看破生死誠不易，

　　　　　　　　　　　　　道經數卷相與析。

　　　　　　　　　　　　　細繹微言參大義，

　　　　　　　　　　　　　毋庸患得又患失。

（白）你好好研讀《太平經》，仔細想想吧。小道會再
來探望，公子保重。

慕容白：多謝道長。

　　　　（南平王、慕容白拱手作別。南平王步出牢房，示意公
　　　　差鎖門）

南平王：此事有些蹊蹺……

　　　　（行至門口，遇到正要入獄探監的盧述）

盧述：　咦，這位道長，請留步。

　　　　（上下打量）您好像不是本地人？

南平王：哦，小道剛打北邊來，聽說這裡有個水陸建醮法會……

盧述：　著啊！您打北邊來，有沒有聽說咱們王爺的消息啊？

南平王：沒有。您是不是知道些什麼？

盧述：　有人說他跟東華王在一起；又有人說，他在北唐。您想
　　　　他到底在哪兒？

南平王：小道不知，只能恭祝王爺平安。

盧述：　哈！是他異想天開，偷偷溜到國外，到處要飯，其實他
　　　　哪是那塊料？（嘲諷）現在安大人代理得很好；他執法
　　　　嚴厲……

南平王：是該嚴厲些。

盧述：　不過，要是他對風流罪稍微放鬆一點兒，也無傷大雅。
　　　　他在那方面實在太苛刻了。

南平王：而今社會風氣淫靡，要嚴厲些才能改善。

盧述：　話雖是這麼說，但是，道長，「食、色，性也」，這種
　　　　事是不可能完全禁止的嘛，除非叫人也不吃飯！（壓低
　　　　嗓門）您看，這個安其樂多麼殘酷啊，只為了人家褲襠
　　　　子裡造反，就要人家的命！（大聲）要是王爺回來就好

了。真希望王爺回來！（看看左右，壓低嗓門）這個陰陽怪氣的代理人，會害國家斷子絕孫的。換成那失蹤的王爺，會這樣做麼？

南平王：您說呢？

盧述：咱們這個王爺啊，嘿嘿！（壓低嗓門）是懂門道的；他享受過這一行的服務。所以，（大聲）他心腸軟。

南平王：小道從未聽過有人指控南平王性好漁色。他不是那種人。

盧述：哈，道長，你被騙啦。王爺這個人哪，（壓低嗓門）暗地裡偷雞摸狗，自會暗中擺平。你不知道他在怡春院的老相好有多少。前兩個月，咱們還一起去逛窰子呢。（大聲）王爺知道我把春嬌的肚子搞大了，也沒說什麼。

南平王：不可能。

盧述：什麼不可能？哼！天下沒有不可能的事。我告訴你，王爺還好酒貪杯、私下創了個酒黨呢。

南平王：您這要不是誤會，就是惡意中傷了。小道所知道的南平王，可是一個明君哪。

盧述：算了，道長，反正我知道自己知道什麼。

南平王：是麼？請問公子尊姓大名？

盧述：我叫盧述，跟王爺是哥倆好。

南平王：好。有機會我會把您呈報上去，相信王爺一定會記得您的。

盧述：哈哈，這是威脅麼？我才不怕你呢。你儘管去呈報，就說是我盧述說的。幸會了，我要去探視朋友了。（下）

南平王：（搖頭苦笑）唉！即使貴為一國之君，也無法禁止市井

　　　的流言誹謗啊！

【伴唱】：有權能令魂魄散，

　　　　　無力管束小人言。

　　　　　即便得意春風面，

　　　　　不堪冷語六月寒。

　　　（切光）

第五場　恫嚇

（地點：公堂議事廳，安其樂踱步沉思）

安其樂：（唱）愁眉深鎖自作苦，

　　　　　　　徹夜難眠神恍惚。

　　　　　　　平生蛾眉閱無數，

　　　　　　　鍾情卻在識面初。

　　　　　　　春色惱人無從訴，

　　　　　　　春雨綿綿有若無。

　　　　　　　不覺報曉催更鼓，

　　　　　（下定決心）放手一搏過河卒！

　　　　　（白）我一向道貌岸然，不假辭色，但現今也顧不得這

　　　　許多了……

　　　　　（一公差上）

公差：　大人，慕容青小姐求見。

安其樂：有請。

公差：　是。（下）

　　　　　（慕容青上，向安其樂施禮，安其樂微微頷首）

慕容青：大人，請問您的決定是？

安其樂：你若知道本官的決定，並願配合，本官會高興得多。令

　　　　弟——不可赦。

慕容青：（稍頓，決心放棄）也罷。願大人洪福齊天。（退後一

　　步，似要離去）

安其樂：但他也可能多活一些時日，甚至更長命。這要看——

慕容青：（又燃起希望）要看您的意思？

安其樂：不，是看**你**的意思。

慕容青：啊？

安其樂：這麼說吧。令弟所犯是無恥之罪，不值得寬宥，就像殺
　　　　人必須償命一樣。

慕容青：可是，大人，舍弟之罪是兩情相悅，並未害人哪。豈能
　　　　與殺人相提並論？

安其樂：是麼？那麼，本官問你：假設——姑且假設有這麼個狀
　　　　況——這兩者你會如何抉擇？——是讓公正的律法立即
　　　　處決令弟，還是，為了救他，獻出自己享受雲雨之歡？

慕容青：大人，我寧可受盡折磨，也不出賣良心。

安其樂：本官不管你的良心。

慕容青：您是說？

安其樂：本官，現在代表明文律令，宣判處死令弟。如果犯罪能
　　　　救令弟一命，這種犯罪難道不是慈悲？

慕容青：當然，如此絕非犯罪，乃是慈悲。您若願發善心，民女
　　　　會早晚為您焚香祝禱，祈求三清尊神庇佑大人。

安其樂：哼！你沒聽懂本官的話。本官再說一遍：假如某人可以
　　　　解救令弟，條件是要你共赴巫山，你會同意麼？

慕容青：大人，我情願赴死，也不能壞了清修。

安其樂：那你不是和律法一樣殘酷麼——眼睜睜看著令弟喪生？

慕容青：大人，法內施仁貴於發乎天性，這與無恥的贖當毫不相

干啊。

安其樂：你先前不是還振振有辭，辯稱令弟的罪行是兩情相悅，
　　　　算不得無恥麼？

慕容青：啊，為了救人，我不得不為他開脫。大人，請原諒我言
　　　　不由衷的懦弱吧。

安其樂：既然你承認自己懦弱，就別一派正經了。

慕容青：民女不明白……大人，您的意思是？

安其樂：好，（意味深長看她一眼）你聽仔細了：
　　　　（唱）為卿銷魂卿知否？
　　　　　　　刻骨相思寤寐求。

慕容青：（一怔）啊？大人您——
　　　　（接唱）信口開呵太荒謬，
　　　　　　　　君無戲言宜好修。

安其樂：（接唱）肺腑之言心應口，
　　　　　　　　一夜春宵釋罪囚。

慕容青：（接唱）清虛自然道德守，
　　　　　　　　苟合非禮應知羞。

安其樂：（接唱）如若誠心將弟救，
　　　　　　　　春風一度解百憂。

慕容青：（接唱）別具肺腸世罕有，
　　　　　　　　道不相同不為謀。
　　　　（白）哈！安其樂，原來你是個陰險的偽君子！你立刻
　　　　發布赦免令，不然，我就要向大家揭發你的真面目。

安其樂：（冷笑）哼、哼！去啊！去揭發啊！誰會相信你呢？本

官崇隆的聲望和地位，會讓你的指控變成誹謗，替你自己招來牢獄之災。得了，別吊本官的胃口了；乖乖順從我。否則——依我現在的想法，令弟不只要被處死，還要遭受凌遲之苦。哼！明日來回話。

（拂袖下）

慕容青：啊！天哪！我能向誰控訴？誰會相信我？這個卑鄙可恨的安其樂！

（唱）居廟堂仗權勢威脅利誘，

　　　　代攝政趁人危予取予求。

　　　　欺世人假正經一絲不苟，

　　　　有誰知他竟是無恥之尤。

　　　　動邪念赴巫山啟人疑竇，

　　　　問所以細尋思好沒來由。

（慕容青來回踱步，忽而俯首自視，忽而駐足遐想）

【伴唱】：莫不是素妝容牽引挑逗，

　　　　貞靜女更勝似嬌媚回眸？

　　　　莫不是好言語未及深究，

　　　　急切切表錯情招來隱憂？

慕容青：（氣惱）這身素服何嘗關情！我又何嘗有一言半語暗示於他！事態如此，真真豈有此理……

（接唱）我豈能將名節輕拋腦後，

　　　　又惟恐他不肯善罷干休。

　　　　恨只恨偽君子上下其手，

　　　　倒教我智慮竭莫展一籌。

　　　　（慕容青似乎凝視遠方，陷入沉思中）

【伴唱】：昊天罔極曷悠悠，

　　　　　悲莫悲兮愁上愁。

　　　　　何去何從沉吟久，

　　　　　萬般滋味在心頭。

慕容青：（已然決定）也罷！性命事小，名節事大。我現在就去
　　　　看白弟，告訴他我的決定。

　　　　（切光）

（中場休息）

第六場　指點

（地點：表演區 A：慕容白牢房。表演區 B：牢獄偏廳。表演區 C：符小姐莊園）

（表演區 A：慕容白牢房）
（喬裝成道長的南平王正與慕容白論道）

南平王：……所以，道常無欲，亦無所求。

慕容白：多謝道長指點迷津。

（典大人引慕容青上）

典大人：文道長，這位是慕容公子的姐姐。

慕容青：（施禮）道長，請容我和舍弟單獨談談。

南平王：（還禮）請。

（南平王、典大人前行數步）

南平王：典大人，小道想聽聽他們說些什麼。請讓我藏在隱密之處。

典大人：請隨我來。

（二人下）

慕容白：姐姐，可有什麼好消息麼？

慕容青：唉，白弟，這位攝政爺要跟玉皇大帝打交道，琢磨著派你去呢。

慕容白：（狐疑）意思是——？

慕容青：意思是——要處決你。

慕容白：（頹然）啊……

慕容青：除非……

慕容白：（眼睛一亮，握住姐姐的手）除非什麼？

慕容青：唉，白弟啊——

　　　　（唱）我與你手足情深朝夕伴，

　　　　　　　綠窗前談文論藝笑語歡。

　　　　　　　只盼你克紹箕裘宏圖展，

　　　　　　　琴瑟和鳴締良緣。

　　　　　　　可嘆那造化弄人命運舛，

　　　　　　　繁華如夢好景難。

　　　　　　　攝政他衣冠禽獸拋顏面，

　　　　　　　為姐我縱然有口也難言。

　　　　　　　無奈何揮淚別弟心悽慘，

　　　　　　　從今後立志修道水雲間。

慕容白：姐姐，你別打啞謎啊！咱們姐弟倆還有什麼不好說的？
　　　　這位攝政爺堂堂正正，怎麼又會是衣冠禽獸呢？

慕容青：（激動）他堂堂正正？對，他是個堂堂正正的大惡棍！
　　　　所有的人，包括王爺，都被他蒙騙了。你知道嗎？他同
　　　　意赦免你，但卻有個荒誕不稽的無恥條件。

慕容白：哦？什麼條件？

慕容青：如果為姐答應了這個條件，即使能保全你的性命，你也
　　　　會痛不欲生的。這種良心上的終生監禁，可是比斬首還
　　　　要殘酷的刑罰啊。而我，更無法苟活於世。

慕容白：到底是什麼條件，你說清楚呀。

慕容青：只要我——獻出貞操，你就可以存活。

慕容白：天哪！不可能。

慕容青：但事實就是如此。如果只是要我的性命，我大可為你犧牲。白弟啊，人生在世，令譽為重。凡事應有所為，有所不為。利用淫行來偷生，這是絕不可取的。

慕容白：啊，姐姐！

慕容青：待等王爺回來，我一定會為你申告。

慕容白：姐！

慕容青：白弟！

　　　　（二人執手對泣）

慕容白：（忽然想到什麼）青姐，難道攝政爺也有人欲？竟能使他在執法之時，枉顧律法來量刑？那麼……

慕容青：怎麼，白弟？

慕容白：姐姐，你想想，攝政爺既然會提出這種條件，不就表示雲雨偷歡實在算不得什麼了不得的大罪麼？

慕容青：白弟，你……

慕容白：哎呀，青姐啊——

　　　　（唱）人死不知何所往，

　　　　　　　孽鏡臺前無可藏。

　　　　　　　黃沙遍野迷霧障，

　　　　　　　魂魄悠悠、從此散八荒。

慕容青：你究竟要說什麼啊？

慕容白：姐姐——

　　　　（接唱）魂魄散，兩相忘，

> 陰陽阻隔斷人腸。
>
> 寒冰刺骨刀山上，
>
> 銅柱火燒鐵板床。
>
> 反覆折磨不忍講，
>
> 愈思愈想——好死不如賴活強。

慕容青：什麼？你說什麼？

慕容白：姐姐，讓我活下去吧。為了救我，你的犧牲絕不是犯罪，而是高尚的善行啊。

慕容青：天哪！你這畜牲！竟然說出這種話來！你，你……

（唱）枉讀詩書作兒郎，

出言無狀太荒唐。

是非顛倒胡亂想，

忍辱偷生亂綱常。

（白）我沒有你這種弟弟！不要妄想我會再去為你求情！

（接唱）無恥淫亂把命喪，

自作自受也應當。

慕容白：姐姐，請聽我說……

慕容青：哼！不必多言了！你會犯罪可不是偶然失足，你根本就是個無恥小人！你死了也罷。慈悲對你不過是個皮條客！

慕容白：啊，姐姐，你聽我說嘛……

（南平王上）

南平王：小道剛巧聽到二位的言談。

　　（向慕容青）對於此事，小道有個主意，或可與小姐參
　　詳。

慕容青：哦？道長請說。

南平王：來，我們出去再說。

　　（向慕容白）你要專心研修道經，莫再無端妄生意念。

　　（慕容白默然，點頭）

　　（南平王、慕容青步出慕容白的牢房，轉入偏廳）

　　（表演區 B：牢獄偏廳）

南平王：慕容小姐，你這般蕙質蘭心，上天一定會保佑你的。眼
　　下你待如何？

慕容青：道長，我要去回覆那個人面獸心的奸賊，讓他死了心。
　　日後王爺回來，我再去向他申冤。

南平王：如此甚好。不過，安大人必然會迴避你的指控，辯稱並
　　無此事，都是你為了報復而惡意中傷。這麼一來，不僅
　　令弟冤死，你也落得聲名敗壞，安大人卻還可能加官進
　　爵呢。

慕容青：這……

南平王：小道雲遊四處，素喜打抱不平。你若信得過我，小道倒
　　有一條妙計。不但可以解救令弟，維護你的名節，還可
　　以幫助一個蒙受冤屈的可憐小姐。

慕容青：哦？請道長明示。只要問心無愧，我都會遵命而行。

南平王：好。你知道前幾年在海上遇難的符將軍嗎？

慕容青：是的。符將軍功勳彪炳，是本國赫赫有名的重臣啊。

南平王：他的小妹，原本已與安大人訂親。大喜之前，符將軍發生不幸，妝奩也跟著沉沒了。不久，安大人以女方行為不檢為由，退了婚約。

慕容青：啊？竟有此事？

南平王：不錯。那位無辜的符小姐，至今還耽溺於悲痛之中……

（表演區 C 出現符巧茵撫琴，做各式身段）

【伴唱】：絃管歇、笙歌盡，

　　　　　　長日漫漫冷淒淒。

　　　　　　家門遭難失所倚，

　　　　　　淚水洗卻紅胭脂。

符巧茵：（接唱）聊將瑤琴訴心事，

　　　　　　深怕旁人笑我癡。

　　　　　　縱然是百般無奈千般恨，

　　　　　　難忘他絕情也有多情時。

　　　　　　這一縷相思欲寄無從寄，

　　　　　　且隨花飛任東西。

（表演區 C 切光）

慕容青：那也無濟於事啊。

南平王：不，這位符小姐非常癡情，對安大人念念不忘。你去回覆安大人，接受他的要求。同時，提出三個條件：第一，停留時間不可過長；第二，地點必須隱密；第三，要在深夜暗中行事。我自會去勸說符小姐代你赴約。如此，

既可保全你們姐弟，日後王爺回來主持公道，符小姐也不致於吃虧。畢竟他們是未婚夫妻哪。

慕容青：（喜出望外，感激不已）極妙！多謝道長。這個主意極好！我這就去。

南平王：放心吧，一切有我。

（南平王微笑頷首，殷勤送到門外，目送慕容青下）

（切光）

第七場　釋囚

（地點：牢獄）

（向隅牢房）

向隅：　嘿！幹哪一行沒有風險？芥菜子都難免落到繡花針眼兒
　　　　裡。老子一個不小心，就被逮著啦！但進了大牢，嘿嘿，
　　　　跟在自個兒家一樣親切。正應了那句俗話：「獵人進山
　　　　只見禽獸，藥農進山只見藥草」，我這前後左右，瞧來
　　　　瞧去，都是熟客嘛。喏、喏、喏，（伸手亂指觀眾席）
　　　　李掌櫃、張軍爺、宋酷吏、柯公子……唷，大夥兒全到
　　　　齊了……一個也不少……

（典大人與公差上，示意公差打開牢門，放出向隅）

典大人：喂，小子，你能砍人頭麼？

向隅：　哈！砍個大壞蛋的腦袋，當然沒問題；但如是老弱婦孺，
　　　　就該讓座了，怎麼還砍得下手？

典大人：得啦，少貧嘴。攝政爺下令，明日要處斬慕容白。這時
　　　　節不對，咱牢裡的劊子手剛好缺個幫手。你要願意改行，
　　　　就免了你的苦役；要不，就關你二十年。因為你是個拉
　　　　皮條的龜奴。

向隅：　大人，小的情願改行，也不想蹲二十年的苦牢啊。

典大人：好。去叫劊子手來。

（公差下。劊子手何保生上）

何保生：大人，您找我？

典大人：嗯，何保生，這小子打今兒個起就跟著你了。有什麼活兒，你教教他。他原是個龜奴，不能跟你比。

何保生：什麼？龜奴？大人，「山羊不跟豺狼作親戚，老鼠不和貓兒結親家」，他的檔次跟咱不同，會丟咱這行手藝的臉面哪。

向隅：　（搶著說話）喂，這位大哥，請別誤會，小弟是個酒保。喏，用現代話來說，就是「調酒師」。調酒，也是一門艱難的手藝啊。（問觀眾）對吧，各位？

典大人：（向何保生）你將就點兒吧，一時找不到適合的人。去吧，去準備吧。

向隅：　（搶上前，表示親熱）大哥，這砍腦袋有什麼訣竅，您教教我，小弟會認真學習。您對我好，我記牢了，將來您若是需要小弟服務，小弟一定手腳俐落，絕對不會讓您吃虧的……

　　　　（向隅哄著何保生下）

典大人：唉，慕容白……（搖搖頭）

　　　　（南平王上）

南平王：咦？慕容公子的赦免令還沒批下來麼？

典大人：沒有。（狐疑）您認為……會有嗎？

南平王：應該快了。

　　　　（傳來非常急促的敲門聲）

南平王：（喜形於色）來了、來了。

　　　　（一公差上，手持詔令）

公差： 啟稟大人，攝政爺派人送來緊急詔令。

（呈上，下。典大人閱讀詔令。）

南平王：（旁白）這紙赦免令，可是用赦免者自己的罪行換來的呀。

（典大人面露驚詫）

南平王：怎麼了？

典大人：攝政爺此舉頗不尋常。這不是赦免令啊。

南平王：啊？說了些什麼？

典大人：您聽聽——（讀令）「……無論如何，寅時一到，立斬慕容白。卯時一刻，本官要親驗首級。不得有誤。」現在已是丑時三刻……

南平王：這真是出乎意料！

（取過詔令，瀏覽一過）典大人，我們必須想個法子來保全他。

典大人：這個……本官不敢擅自做主。

南平王：（思考片刻，取出玉璽）典大人，你來看，這是什麼？

典大人：啊！鎮國玉璽！這……您是……？

南平王：噤聲！（看看左右）天機不可洩露！

典大人：是、是，微臣明白。（欲下跪）

南平王：（阻攔）免。（收好玉璽）典大人，你看此事應如何處理？

典大人：這……

（二人陷入沉思）

【伴唱】：節外生枝違人願，

> 左思右想事難全。
>
> 步步為營細盤算，
>
> 化險為夷頃刻間。

典大人：（念頭一轉）有了，這牢裡半點鐘前剛死了個山賊，年紀與慕容公子相仿，或許我們可以做點兒手腳，去應付攝政爺？

南平王：（驚喜）啊，此乃天意！就這麼辦。快去！

典大人：是。

南平王：慢！你還要找個處所，把慕容白藏起來。過兩日，便知分曉。快去！

典大人：是。（下）

　　　　（南平王略一思索，伏案振筆疾書，封好）

　　　　（一公差引慕容青上，公差即下）

慕容青：（施禮）道長，舍弟的赦免令送來了麼？

南平王：（起身還禮）慕容小姐，安大人方才下令釋放他——

慕容青：（欣喜）是真的？

南平王：真的。安大人讓他永遠脫離凡塵。——他已被處決了。

慕容青：（不可置信）啊？可是，符小姐已然赴約回來，怎會如此？

南平王：不幸正是如此。

慕容青：（憤慨）哦！可憐的白弟！這個萬惡不赦的安其樂！

　　　　（唱）機關算盡太可恨，

　　　　　　一手遮天欺煞人。

　　　　　　信誓旦旦猶在耳，

　　　　　　不過須臾骨肉分。

　　　　　　賊子背信比狼狠，

　　　　　　教我喑啞黃連吞。

　　　　　　心如刀割淚難禁，

　　　　　　忍無可忍、定要把冤申！

　　（掩面痛哭）

南平王：（冷靜）好了，別哭了。注意聽我說：根據可靠的消息，
　　　　王爺明日就回來了。來！（上前牽起慕容青之手，轉身
　　　　取過案頭信函）你拿著這封信函，去沖虛觀找丘道長，
　　　　就說是我的主意，讓他明日未時帶著你和符小姐去城門
　　　　口攔道喊冤。其他的事，小道自會妥善安排。

慕容青：（狐疑；拭淚）是，道長。

南平王：（堅定）王爺一定會給你們應得的公道。

　　　　（拍拍慕容青的肩，溫柔）相信我。放心吧！一切有我。

慕容青：多謝道長。　（下）

南平王：（唱）君子為政須行善，

　　　　　　至誠無息萬象含。

　　　　　　一日三省蒼生念，

　　　　　　素位而行天下安。

　　　　　　量刑不忘通權變，

　　　　　　深思熟慮懲罪愆。

　　　　　　豈容鑽營好手段？

　　　　　　瞞天過海情何堪！

　　　　　　撥亂返正不容緩，

（句末）

目看雲——問看巧說時運蹇。

第八場　量·度

（地點：南平王國城門口）

安其樂：　（唱）我本是棟梁材參贊中樞，

行得端坐得正不同流俗。

只因為一念差進退維谷，

言無信鑄大錯罪不容誅。

縱然是用心計掩人耳目，

也難防山窮盡水落石出。

而今是亂如麻六神無主，

愧無語問蒼天悔不當初。

（白）唉！希望這位玉潔冰清的小姐，會由於羞愧失貞，或是震懾於我的威權，而不敢聲張。……唉！應該饒他一命的。就怕他血氣方剛，嚥不下這口氣，留下無窮後患。……天哪！我這是怎麼了？難道少了悲憫，就什麼都不成了麼？

天哪！

（權世可與百官、群眾上）

權世可、百官：大人！

安其樂：啊！列位大人！

（眾人行禮如儀，分別列隊。安其樂、權世可率百官恭迎王爺入城，眾百姓夾道歡呼，盧述也來湊熱鬧）

安其樂：權大人，王爺前兩日不是派人傳話，說他還在西岐，一時之間不克回來麼？

權世可：正是。這幾日接二連三傳來的消息都不同，老臣也猜不透這箇中玄機。

安其樂：王爺的旨意，前後矛盾，教人好生納悶。此一手諭，竟特別指示要在城門口開放百姓陳情。權大人，依你之見，這……

權世可：大人，老臣以為，為了慎重其事，還是遵照手諭辦理為是。老臣昨日已派人四下張貼告示，鳴鑼布達此一訊息。

　　　　（公差上）

公差：　報！王爺回城了！

南平王：（內唱）風塵僕僕陽關道，

　　　　（南平王匆匆策馬上）

　　　　（接唱）快馬加鞭不辭勞。

　　　　　　　胸有成竹煙塵掃，

　　　　　　　正本清源在今朝。

安其樂、權世可率百官：（上前）臣等恭迎王爺。

南平王：（下馬，向安、權二人）二位辛苦了。本王在歸途中早已聽聞二位嚴明公正的風評。二位真是本王得力的左右手，應予褒揚。

安其樂、權世可：王爺過獎，臣等不敢居功。

安其樂：微臣不過忠君之事，恪守本分而已。

南平王：哈哈！愛卿忒過謙了！

　　　　（丘道長、慕容青上）

丘道長：就是現在；去吧。

慕容青：（上前，下跪）冤枉啊！王爺！求求您，請為民女慕容
　　　　青主持公道、公道、公道！

南平王：哦？你有何冤屈？安大人在此，他會給你公道。你就對
　　　　他陳情吧。

慕容青：啊，王爺容稟，您這是讓我找閻王拿藥單哪。請您親自
　　　　審理吧。求求您！

安其樂：王爺，這是個瘋子。她曾為了兄弟向我求情，但其弟已
　　　　依法處決……

慕容青：（倏然站起）依法！依法？

安其樂：她的言語一定反覆無常、匪夷所思。

慕容青：王爺，民女所控訴的一切似乎匪夷所思，實則不然。

　　　　（指著安其樂）他——

　　　　（唱）安其樂，偽君子！

　　　　　　　蒙上欺下假公濟私。

　　　　　　　預謀殺人真卑鄙，

　　　　　　　玷辱處子倒行逆施。

南平王：嗯，果然匪夷所思。

　　　　來人，把她帶走，她顯然是精神錯亂。

　　　　（二公差上前）

慕容青：不，王爺——

　　　　（接唱）看似荒唐一場戲，

　　　　　　　　句句實言非無稽。

　　　　（南平王揮手，示意公差退下）

慕容青：有些齷齪小人，總是彬彬有禮。還有些人衣冠楚楚，但
卻是憝惡元凶啊。王爺啊——

　　　　（唱）天下世事多矛盾，

　　　　　　　知人知面難知心。

　　　　　　　亂臣賊子貌恭謹，

　　　　　　　色屬內荏假殷勤。

　　　　　　　自應持平細究論，

　　　　　　　明察秋毫識本真。

南平王：（向安其樂、權世可）她的陳述有條不紊，看來不像瘋
子——雖然本王相信她瘋了。

　　　　（向左右）去取兩把座椅來。

　　　　（左右安置座椅。南平王攜安其樂上坐）

　　　　（向慕容青）好吧，你有何冤情？

慕容青：民女是慕容白的姐姐，舍弟因姦淫罪被安其樂判處斬
刑。民女那時正在修真觀參法修習，舍弟請託一位盧迷
公子前來報信——

盧迷：　（上前插話）稟王爺，就是小民。接著，小民就陪同這
位小姐去請求安大人的赦免。

慕容青：正是。

南平王：（向盧迷）本王沒有問你。

盧迷：　是，王爺，但您也沒叫我閉嘴啊。

南平王：多口！該你陳述時，你最好不要結巴。

盧迷：　小民保證不會。

南平王：保證？小心你的偽證吧。

（向慕容青）說下去。

慕容青：我去見這位卑劣惡毒的攝政⋯⋯

南平王：（向安其樂）這又是瘋言瘋語了。

慕容青：簡而言之，民女再三求懇後，（指安其樂）此人，竟然
提出無恥的要求——

南平王：哦？什麼要求？

慕容青：王爺——他——他要民女奉獻貞操，作為舍弟免死的條
件。經過天人交戰，姐弟情深更勝於我的名譽。因此，
民女屈服於他。然而，滿足了他的淫欲後，他卻立刻下
令處斬了舍弟。

南平王：荒唐！這是六朝志怪麼？你太異想天開了！

慕容青：王爺，民女不敢妄言。這是千真萬確的呀！

南平王：你若不是瘋子，就是有人教唆。你知道誹謗朝廷命官，
該當何罪嗎？安大人的廉明公正，有目共睹。設若他果
真如你所言，犯下姦淫之罪，那他應會設身處地、多方
考量而赦免令弟。

說！這些胡言亂語，究竟是哪個教唆於你的？從實招
來！

慕容青：既然王爺不信，也就罷了！民女只能祈求上天垂憐！（欲
下）

南平王：且慢！本王豈容他人任意誹謗本王的愛卿？來人，把她
抓起來。

（二公差上，抓住慕容青）

這裡頭一定有什麼陰謀。說！是誰教你來的？

慕容青：有位文道長，可惜他不在此。

南平王：押下去，聽候發落。

　　　　（二公差押解慕容青下）

　　　　好個道長！哼，你們有誰認得那個文道長？

盧述：　回稟王爺，小民認得。那個道長吃飽了撐著，很愛管閒
　　　　事。前兩日我在牢獄門口碰到他，他還大放厥詞，批評
　　　　王爺您呢。他若不是個道長，我真想給他幾個耳刮子。

南平王：批評我？哼，膽子不小！去，把這個道長帶來。

　　　　（二公差下）

丘道長：啟稟王爺，小道對於此事略知一二。其實，這位小姐不
　　　　該控訴安大人，因為她是清白的；安大人根本沒有侵犯
　　　　她。小道可以證明這一點。

南平王：哦？這有意思。你且證明給本王看。

丘道長：是。請稍候。（下）

南平王：（向安其樂）愛卿，你看，庶民無知，一至於此！此事
　　　　本王絕不偏祖，你自己來斷自己的案吧。

　　　　（丘道長引蒙面的符巧茵上）

南平王：這位可是人證，道長？讓她先揭去面紗再說。

符巧茵：王爺，請原諒民女暫時必須蒙面。我要等候夫君的吩咐。

南平王：哦？你已嫁為人婦了麼？

符巧茵：沒有。

南平王：那你是閨女囉？

符巧茵：不是。

南平王：是寡婦麼？

符巧茵：也不是。

南平王：咦，那你什麼都不是麼？

盧述：　王爺，她可能是妓女啊。

南平王：多口！待會兒自有你說話的時候。

盧述：　是。（吐吐舌頭）

符巧茵：回稟王爺，是這樣的：民女已與夫君圓房，但他並不知情。

　　　　（眾人笑）

南平王：這是何故？

盧述：　那傢伙喝醉了嘛！

南平王：（向盧述）你再多口，就先給你二十大板！

　　　　（盧述縮脖，雙手迅即摀嘴）

　　　　（向符巧茵）好吧。言歸正傳，你不是要為安大人作證麼？

符巧茵：是的，王爺。控訴他犯姦淫罪的那位小姐，也同樣控訴了我夫君。但民女發誓，她所指控的時辰，我夫君正與我共享魚水之歡。

安其樂：怎麼？她不只控訴我一人？

符巧茵：據我所知沒有旁人。

南平王：咦，那你的夫君呢？

符巧茵：王爺，那就是安其樂大人。

安其樂：是可忍、孰不可忍？你是何人？取下面紗來。

符巧茵：是，謹遵夫君之命。

　　　　（取下面紗）

您還認得我麼？

南平王：（向安其樂）你認識她麼？

安其樂：是，微臣認識。不瞞王爺，微臣曾與她訂親，但早已解
　　　　除婚約。這三年來，我不曾與她說過一言半語。王爺，
　　　　這些人必定是受了挑撥，或許後頭還隱藏著更大的陰
　　　　謀，請容我查明真相。

南平王：如此甚好。愛卿，你就看著辦吧。
　　　　（南平王起身離座，向權世可）權大人，勞駕你上座。
　　　　（權世可坐定，南平王向安、權二人）二位辛苦些，今
　　　　日務必要查個清楚，好好懲處這些誣告者。本王另有要
　　　　事，去去就來。

安其樂、權世可：（起身恭送）是，王爺慢走。臣等定當澈底查
　　　　辦。
　　　　（南平王下）

安其樂：（向符巧茵）哪個指使你來污衊本官的？也是那個文道
　　　　長麼？

符巧茵：是文道長指點的，但我一切均據實稟告。大人，夫君，
　　　　你這薄倖郎啊——
　　　　（唱）畫堂深靜無人處，
　　　　　　　花前月下定情初。
　　　　　　　海誓山盟多戀慕，
　　　　　　　媒證尚有雙明珠。
　　　　　　　可嘆恩情實難卜，
　　　　　　　一朝棄置我何辜？

　　　　　心如蓮子常含苦，

　　　　　人前歡笑背人哭。

　　　　　惆悵無計留春住，

　　　　　夜夜繡帷燒紅燭。

　　　　　頻問玉籠小鸚鵡，

　　　　　相思兩字怎生書、怎生書？

　　　（飲泣、拭淚）

安其樂：呀，你這賤人——

　　　（唱）叨叨絮絮自取辱，

　　　　　胡亂編派巧言誣。

　　　　　不由本官惱又怒，

　　　　　傷風敗俗脫口出。

權世可：帶慕容青。

　　　（對安其樂）大人且寬心，由本官來訊問她。讓她們兩個對質，必能查出真相。

　　　（二公差押解慕容青上，另二公差引喬裝成道長的南平王上）

權世可：喂，你就是文道長麼？

南平王：正是。

盧述：　就是這個傢伙，一點兒不錯！

權世可：你為何教唆這兩個瘋女人來誹謗安其樂大人？她們已經承認了。

南平王：胡說八道！

權世可：放肆！你知道這是公堂問案麼？

南平王：這是什麼公堂！王爺在哪裡？小道要親稟王爺。

權世可：王爺現在由安大人和本官代理。你要老老實實的，不然
　　　　就先治你一個藐視公堂的大罪。

南平王：啊，王爺離開了麼？

　　　　（向慕容、符二人）那你們還申什麼冤、告什麼狀啊？
　　　　王爺不公不義，竟把你們的冤案交給惡棍來審理。你們
　　　　原本就是來此指控他的呀。

盧述：　（上前插話）大人，這就是那個無賴。您看他那德行！

權世可：可惡！你不但教唆這兩個瘋女人來誣告朝廷命官，還敢
　　　　辱罵王爺！拖下去，先打四十大板！

南平王：哼！別忙。即使是王爺本人，也不敢動我一根汗毛。小
　　　　道不是本地人，雲遊至此，眼見人心荒淫，法紀廢弛，
　　　　真是一副衰敗之象。

權世可：喝，污衊朝廷，應該打入大牢。

安其樂：且慢。盧公子，你有什麼要指控他的麼？

盧述：　是啊，大人。——過來，你這傲慢的道士，你認得我吧？

南平王：哦，是你啊。咱們在牢獄裡見過。

盧述：　沒錯。那你還記得自己是怎麼批評王爺的麼？

南平王：批評王爺？

盧述：　是啊。你那時口沫橫飛，左一個嫖客，右一個懦夫，羞
　　　　辱王爺，還直稱他是個傻蛋……

南平王：哦，那不是小道說的。恰好相反，都是你說的，還有更
　　　　多的惡言惡語。

盧述：　噢，你這禿驢！睜眼說瞎話。我當時不是還氣得拽你耳

朵麼？

南平王：小道可要鄭重聲明：我愛王爺一如愛我自個兒。

安其樂：這個大逆不道的無賴，還敢狡辯！

權世可：根本不必多費唇舌。來人哪！把他打入大牢。還有那兩
　　　　　個瘋子、一個共犯。

　　　　　（若干公差上，抓住慕容、符、丘）

南平王：急什麼？慢著！

盧述：　哈，你敢反抗？

　　　　　（盧述上前幫忙公差）

　　　　　（混亂中，南平王的帽子被盧述扯落）

安其樂、權世可：（發現這是南平王，立即起身，驚呼）王爺！

　　　　　（眾人面面相覷）

安其樂、權世可：（偕眾人下跪）王爺恕罪！

南平王：平身。

　　　　　（眾人起）

　　　　　（向盧述）哼，好傢伙，敢在太歲頭上動土。

　　　　　（交代公差）把他抓起來。

　　　　　（向盧述）等一下那個道士要好好跟你算這筆賬。

盧述：　這下慘了！（拍拍頭）咱的腦袋……

　　　　　（二公差上，抓住盧述，帶到一旁。丘道長捧上王冠，
　　　　　南平王整理衣冠）

南平王：（上坐，指著慕容、符、丘）先釋放他們。

　　　　　（向權世可）權大人，本王寬恕你。你且坐下。

　　　　　（權世可坐下，安其樂立於一旁）

　　　　至於安大人嘛，（向安其樂）現在，你還有何臉面、有
　　　　何言語？

安其樂：啊——

　　　　（旁唱）王爺他智謀高出其不意，

　　　　　　　　愧無顏再辯解百感交集。

　　　　　　　　一步差步步差作法自斃，

　　　　　　　　七尺軀仰天嘆死不足惜。

　　　　（白）王爺，罪臣無話可說。如再隱瞞，就是罪上加罪。
　　　　請勿再審，且容我認罪，直接處斬吧。

南平王：那好。符巧茵，近前——你與她訂過親麼？

安其樂：是。

南平王：押下去，讓他倆即刻完婚。權大人，你去主婚。事畢再
　　　　把他們帶回來。

權世可：是。

　　　　（權世可、符巧茵、二公差押解安其樂下）

南平王：（向慕容青）慕容小姐，道長雖然改作王爺，並不因換
　　　　了衣裳就改了心腸，我還是一樣關注於你。

慕容青：噢，王爺，請原諒民女有眼不識泰山，增添了這許多麻
　　　　煩。

南平王：本王赦免你，但你對本王也要同樣寬容。我原以為令弟
　　　　的行刑不會如此迅速，以致措手不及。

慕容青：唉，那是他自己命薄福淺，豈能怪罪王爺？

南平王：你能這般設想，再好不過。

　　　　（權世可、符巧茵、二公差押解安其樂上，權世可歸座）

南平王：安其樂，你知法犯法在前，毀約背信在後。奪人貞操，毀人名節，瞞上欺下，罪不可逭。你應知「種什麼因，結什麼果」。本王就「以子之道，還治子身」；你怎麼量，本王也怎麼度！現在判你斬刑；而且要跟處決慕容白一樣迅速執行。

符巧茵：（大驚，急忙下跪）啊，仁慈的王爺，請勿賜給民女一個名不副實的夫君哪。

南平王：本王曾允諾保障你的名譽與權利，因此依法賜婚。而他的家產，本應沒收充公，不過，本王格外開恩，交由你全部繼承。如你願意，本王可再為你另配良緣。

符巧茵：噢，不，好心的王爺，民女不願再醮。

南平王：不必多言；本王心意已決。

符巧茵：慈悲的好王爺……

南平王：多言無益！押下去。

符巧茵：求求您啊！慈悲的好王爺……

（向慕容青）噢，好心的慕容姐姐，幫幫我啊。求求您，幫我向王爺求情啊。求求您給他一個重新做人的機會吧。求求您……

南平王：（冷峻）他必須為慕容白償命。

符巧茵：慕容姐姐，您不用開口，只要陪我跪著……

南平王：她若下跪，如何對得起她冤死的弟弟？她弟弟在九泉之下，豈能瞑目？

慕容青：（注視符巧茵，再注視安其樂。緩緩下跪。語氣堅定）王爺，請您刀下留人吧。畢竟──舍弟確有過失。依法

論法，也是無可厚非。至於安其樂的邪念——其實並未得逞，姑且就當作未曾發生吧。民女以為，他原先也是執意守法，只是後來見到了我……。王爺啊，請您寬大為懷——

（唱）人非聖賢孰能無過？

　　　　知過能改善莫大焉。

　　　　舍弟伏法時乖命舛，

　　　　咎由自取理亦當然。

　　　　仁君居位防微杜漸，

　　　　不教而殺是謂暴殘。

　　　　博施於民取長補短，

　　　　咨諏善道察納雅言。

　　　　假以時日耳濡目染，

　　　　河清海晏少懷老安。

南平王：（深受感動，旁白）呀，慕容白之掉包計，本王故意秘而不宣，原是有心試探於她。她這番話——

　　　　（旁唱）娓娓道來引經據典，

　　　　　　　　言近旨遠器識不凡。

　　　　　　　　心懷慈惠以德報怨，

　　　　　　　　審時度勢才貌雙全。

　　　　　　　　當頭棒喝殷鑑不遠，

　　　　　　　　從今往後任人唯賢。

　　　　　　　　且依所請網開一面，

　　　　　　　　翻手新譜宿世良緣。

（白）你們都起來吧。本王自會定奪。典大人呢？

（符巧茵、慕容青二人站起）

典大人：（上前）微臣在。

南平王：為何慕容白的行刑時間不合慣例？你知罪麼？

典大人：是、是，微臣知罪。

南平王：（故意地）為此，本王要降你三級，罰俸一年。

典大人：謝王爺，但微臣處理此案另有權宜之策，且人證、物證
俱全。

南平王：哦？呈上來。

典大人：是，遵命。

（典大人揮手，一公差帶蒙面的慕容白上）

典大人：稟王爺，此即鐵證。

（典大人揭開慕容白的面巾，眾人驚訝，交頭接耳）

慕容青：（驚呼）白弟！

慕容白：姐姐！

（姐弟二人相擁而泣）

南平王：本王赦免慕容白，也赦免安其樂。

（向慕容白）你要儘早擇日完婚。

（向安其樂）你要改過自新。

（指著慕容白、安其樂）你們死裡逃生，要謹記這次的
教訓，不可再犯。日後夫唱婦隨，相敬如賓。

慕容白、安其樂：謝王爺。

南平王：（看看盧述）只有一個人——不得原諒。

（向盧述）現在輪到你了。誹謗本王，你知罪麼？

盧述：　啊，仁慈的好王爺，小民不過跟著《芒果日報》爆料，
　　　　順口胡謅兩句，您大人大量，千萬莫當真哪。

南平王：本王可以寬恕你的誹謗，但你必須明媒正娶那個為你害
　　　　喜的春嬌姑娘，立為正室。

盧述：　天啊！好王爺，求求您，行行好！不要叫我娶妓女當元
　　　　配啊！不然，這等於是笞杖加凌遲，比處斬還要悲慘哪。

南平王：誹謗本王該當此刑。押下去！你非娶不可。

　　　　（二公差押盧述下）

盧述：　（邊走邊喊）誰來替我說說好話啊？莎士比亞大爺⋯⋯

南平王：權大人、典大人，二位用心公務、處置得宜，本王將另
　　　　行論功行賞。

權、典二人：謝王爺。

南平王：慕容小姐，本王尚有一言——

　　　　（走向慕容青）

　　　　（唱）卿如紅梅凝雪釀，

　　　　　　　晶瑩玉潤十里香。

　　　　　　　天姿靈秀心透亮，

　　　　　　　襟抱別有好文章。

　　　　　　　難得寬厚大處想，

　　　　　　　儀範天下柔克剛。

　　　　　　　問卿可願中宮掌，

　　　　　　　共效于飛龍鳳祥？

慕容青：　（非常意外）啊？這⋯⋯

南平王：（溫柔）此事不忙，稍後再談。

（吩咐左右）來人哪，擺駕回宮。

（眾人依序下。慕容青獨留原地，若有所思）

（切光）

尾　聲

（地點：南平王國市衢大道）

（公差上，張貼告示。眾百姓圍觀。南平王率權世可等
上，與眾人閒話家常，一派和樂繁榮）

【伴唱】：廢嚴刑、乾坤轉，
　　　　　恩威並濟舉大端。
　　　　　細察民隱真偽辨，
　　　　　選賢與能舉世歡。
　　　　　以己度人識見淺，
　　　　　激濁揚清要從權。
　　　　　心存悲憫蒼生念，
　　　　　休休有容天地寬。

劇　終

Selected Scores

精選曲譜

天道好生
How Very Dear
慕容青唱

作曲 耿玉卿
配器 李宏權

君子任德 不

任 刑 歸真返璞遵古訓

教化為 先 無棄

人

六慾沒主張　可憐

我　　坐立難安

癡　癡　想

心猿意馬

好彷徨　　　　　　此情

此景俱難忘　是　殺

是赦　費思

量　　　　　　　費思量

六和
The Whole Wide World
南平王唱

作曲 耿玉卿
配器 李宏權

·69·

愁眉深鎖
My Brows Knitted
安其樂唱

作曲　耿玉卿
配器　李宏權

愁　眉

深

鎖　　　　　　　　自　作　苦

夜　難　眠　　神　　　恍　惚

放 手 一 搏 一 搏 p

遏 河 卒

昊 天 罔 極　　　　曷 悠 悠

悲 莫 悲 兮　　　愁 上 愁　　　何 去

何 從　沉 吟　　久 _p_　　　　　萬 般

滋　　味　　　在　　心

頭　　　　　　在 心 頭

君子爲政
A King Does Well
南平王唱

作曲 耿玉卿
配器 李宏權

♩=76

罪 愆　　豈 容 鑽

營　好 手 段 瞞 天 過 海 情

何 堪　撥 亂 反 正　不

容 緩 且　　看

我

鬥 智 巧　　設

計　　連

環

我本是棟梁材
An Eminent Member
安其樂唱

作曲 耿玉卿
配器 李宏權

亂　　如麻　　六　神無

主　　　　　　　　　　愧無語問　蒼

天　　　　　　　　　　　　　　　　　　_p_

悔不當　　初

悔　不當

初

畫堂深靜
In Quiet Painted Hall

符巧茵唱

作曲　耿玉卿
配器　李宏權

苦訴　♩=76

弹拨　民乐入

Voice

畫 堂 深 靜 無 人 處

p

花 前 月 下

定 情 初 海 誓 山 盟 多 戀 慕

媒 證 尚 有 雙 明 珠

V

p 可 嘆 恩 情

實 難 p 一 朝

棄 置 我 何 辜 心 如 蓮 子 常 含

圖 1 王海玲飾南平王(Hai-Ling Wang as The Prince)

圖 2 王海玲飾文道長(Hai-Ling Wang as Priest Wen)

圖 3　蕭揚玲飾慕容青(Yang-Ling Hsiao as Murong Qing)

圖 4　劉建華飾安其樂(Chian-Hua Liu as An Qilo)

圖 5 朱海珊飾權世可(Hai-Shan Chu as Quan Shike)

圖 6 安其樂(左)與慕容青(An Qilo, left, and Murong Qing)

圖 7 南平王(左)與慕容青(The Prince, left, and Murong Qing)

圖 8 (從左至右)安其樂、南平王與權世可
(left to right: An Qilo, The Prince, and Chuan Shike)